Under the Tracks

The Douglas Town Chronicles
1 Book 1 2

By Ginger G. Howard

First Edition

ISBN: 978-0-578-96371-6
Publisher: Gemini Pacific Publishing

Edited by: Angie Gia-Bennett, Todd Downing, and Paul Howard

Cover Design: Copyright© 2021 Riley M. Howard

We meet them at the door-way, on the stair,
Along the passages they come and go,
Impalpable impressions on the air,
A sense of something moving to and fro.

There are more guests at table than the hosts
Invited; the illuminated hall
Is thronged with quiet, inoffensive ghosts,
As silent as the pictures on the wall.

Excerpt from *Haunted Houses* written in 1858
By Henry Wadsworth Longfellow

{ Prologue }

We stood side by side, with our gaze facing upward in contemplation of the long trek ahead. We must have been quite the sight to cars passing by, with our backs to the freeway as the heat radiated off of the cement in the warm mid-morning sun.

"Remind me again why we are doing this, Gwen?"

Four years earlier...

As a child, my summer birthday tradition was to spend the day at the Douglas Zoo. Besides just loving animals I liked how the zoo had a feeling of untouched wilderness. Its exhibits followed the gentle rise and fall of the hilltop and much of the surrounding woodland had been left intact. High on my list of to-dos while there was to ride the miniature zoo train through the surrounding forest.

The train was a replica of a late 1800s steam engine, complete with a conductor dressed in overalls and cap. The whole thing was painted bright red with green trim, and consisted of an engine that pulled a dozen or so open air passenger cars. Each car had short wooden slats for railings, red benches and a little green metal roof overhead to keep the passengers dry. It did rain a lot in our little town of Douglas, Oregon, but by the time my birthday came around it was usually sunny and warm.

Each time the train departed the depot at the zoo it meandered along the outskirts of the property behind the exhibits, which was off limits to the general public. Then it would head off, away from the main grounds, for a mile long circuit cut through the hills beneath the trees of an old growth forest covering a series of radiating ravines and vegetation choked gullies.

The most exhilarating moment for me was when we disappeared under the thick canopy, and the temperature dropped - a welcome relief from the summer heat. It felt like we were leaving the world behind.

About halfway through the journey there is a point where the tracks curve sharply left, hugging the wall of a deep notch in the terrain. I always thought it looked like the shape of a horseshoe. The track lay atop an artificial terrace, carved into this natural arc, about twenty feet below the hill's summit. If you dared to look out the right side of the train, the cut out dropped steeply away. You could see down into an ocean of trees, reaching up toward the sun, away from the dark forest floor. The forest was so thick that it hid the underlying terrain covered in a blanket of shrubs, ferns, ivy, fungi and moss.

It wasn't a hard stretch of the imagination to see how a child could fall out of the train, if being bold and foolish, and if the parents weren't paying close attention. I always found it a bit anxiety-inducing, gazing down there, the thought of being stranded, covered in the darkness of all the foliage, looking up as the train chugged away... no one noticing I was gone. These thoughts always struck me at that same bend in the track, year after year.

Eventually the rails wound away from the steep drop-off and my *most* favorite part of the ride would come into view - the house.

It stood atop the summit, visible to passengers only if they strained to look up. I always looked up! In its former glory, I imagined it must have been majestic. At this point, however, it was slowly being choked out by tree and shrub overgrowth, the paint was gone, and it looked like it was falling apart.

I was entranced by this old house. I wanted to know who had lived there. What had their lives been like before it was abandoned and the wood started rotting away? What was the view like from the third story tower window?

Every time I asked the train conductor anything, the vague reply was always the same, "That old house has always been a mystery." This answer did not satisfy me at all.

On my tenth birthday, I took what would become my last ride on the zoo train. I had made the mistake of telling my parents what I saw peeking out of the dense foliage, right before we came into the "horseshoe" bend in the tracks.

He was standing down the hill a bit, within the ferns, tucked back in a grove of trees, staring up at me. I asked my mom, "Why is the little boy down there in the forest?"

"What little boy?" My mom asked, looking out of the train car.

"He's right there," I insisted, pointing at the figure fading in and out of view within the shadows. As the train continued on its course, we did not break eye contact, and despite me pointing right at him, no one seemed to be able to see him but me.

Other people on the train had gathered on the right side, also peering out over the railings down into the foliage.

"Did someone fall out of the train?" one father asked.

"Maybe someone should tell the conductor to stop!" a woman yelled.

"He's right there!" I shouted at all the grown-ups, pointing frantically. "Yes, stop the train! Stop the train!" I started to screech at the top of my lungs. I was getting light headed and nauseous. I felt panic rising in my chest, as the train pulled away from him and continued around the bend.

I was beside myself in tears, "We have to go back for him. He's lost. He just wants his mom. He can't find his mom!" I really wasn't sure how I knew this, I just did.

"It's okay Gwen. Just stop yelling. Shhh," my father whispered as he held me on his lap trying to silence my hysterics. "We will tell the conductor when we stop, and they will go back to find him I promise." The nausea began to subside, and my head became clearer.

When we disembarked at the train station, a long fifteen minutes later, my parents told the conductor what I had seen. He walked up to the ticket window at the depot, and a moment later a voice came on over the loud speaker.

"If anyone has any information about a missing child just seen in the forest, please come up to the ticket window immediately. Again, if anyone has any information about a missing child, please come to the ticket window immediately."

Security quickly approached the depot where we were seated. One guard knelt down to my level and asked me a series of questions: "Can you tell us what he looked like? How old was he? Can you tell us what he was wearing?"

Through leaky eyes and a snot filled nose I did my 10-year-old best to answer his questions, as he looked back and forth between me and my parents in confusion. He must have asked me what the boy was wearing at least a dozen times.

I overheard the security guard try to whisper to my father privately, "We've sent out a team to search the forest, but just so you know, we have not had a report of anyone missing today."

"I saw him! He is out there alone. He wants his mom. You need to find his mom!" I screeched again in complete frustration.

Families wandering the zoo, near the area, started to get concerned and ask questions. The management had to have been afraid of the public backlash. If a child managed to wander off and got lost, or worse, fallen out of the train, it would have been very bad publicity, so they moved us to the main office area, out of earshot of the public.

They kept reassuring me that they were looking, but after hours had passed, they found no sign of anyone on the hillside in that section of forest. I heard them tell my parents that they had called off the search.

"Gwen, they are going to let us go home now. It's been a long day," my father said as he came back from talking to people in charge.

"But… what about the boy? Did they find him? Is he okay? Did you find his mom?"

"Honey, everything is fine," my mother said. "Let's get our stuff and head home okay?" My mother said.

"Did you find him? Is he okay?" I asked again, my voicing rising. I was so worried and so frustrated that I felt like screaming at everyone around me.

"They didn't find anyone, Gwen. No one is lost in the forest. You must have been mistaken. But that's okay; it means no one is missing their mommy. It's okay," my mother offered, trying to gather up her purse and hurry us along out of the building.

"I am NOT mistaken!" I yelled, causing everyone around us in the building to turn and stare. "He's still out there! He's still out there!"

My father quickly grabbed my arm, his face a crimson red, anger in his eyes. "Stop yelling! Control yourself. We are going home now!" He yanked hard as he pulled me out of the building. "Stop causing a scene! We will talk about this when we get in the car. Now come on."

All the adults that day concluded the sighting had been a figment of my overactive imagination. The zoo management scolded my parents for all the trouble I had caused, and pretty much made it clear I wasn't invited back. At least that is the impression that I got, that I was the pariah of the park.

I never wavered from my story though, not once. I maintained the fact that I saw what I saw: a boy between the ages of 8-10, standing alone in the forest. He had disheveled short brown hair, a round sunken-in face with dirt streaked across chipmunk cheeks, and dark circles under his eyes. He wore a very loose, stained, off-white shirt with missing buttons up the front. The shirt was half way tucked into short brown pants; pants like the kids on *the Little Rascals* would have worn. It looked like he was trying to say something to me as he pointed his finger towards the ground under the tracks.

The unusually large sleepy brown eyes haunted me every day after that, as if they were pleading with me to understand. With this memory always came the same wave of emotion I felt on the train that day: sadness from a profound loss, like missing someone so badly you wanted to cry from the pain it caused, followed by a bout of light-headedness and nausea.

I stopped sharing these experiences with my parents. It became a taboo subject that I was never to bring up again. I was also told to stop asking to go back to the zoo for my birthday.

"Why can't I go back?" I would ask each year following. "I'll be good this time! I promise I won't *cause a scene.*" I used the phrase they used on me that day.

"It would be too upsetting for you to go back there," they would offer as an excuse. "We'll find something even more fun to do to for your birthday."

I began to wonder if it were more about them wanting to avoid further humiliation. It's not often that the zoo is pretty much turned upside down in a manhunt for a figment of a 10-year-old's so-called imagination.

The sighting was definitely nothing I imagined. It was too real to have been my imagination. I had a lot of years to dwell on this fact, and dream about him nightly. I came to believe that if there was not an actual person lost in that forest that day, then what I saw must have been a *ghost.*

I also often wondered how the boy would have gotten himself stranded in the forest in the first place, if he hadn't fallen off the train. The only logical conclusion, I decided, was that it must have had something to do with the derelict Victorian house. It was, after all, the closest structure in proximity to where the boy was standing. Maybe he and his mother had lived there? Finding a way to someday somehow get to that house became like an obsession.

It took my friends several years of growing up before they believed me. They, like my parents, had thought I made it up. It took them being exposed to enough ghost and supernatural-themed movies and TV shows, before they started to become more open-minded. When puberty came along... BAM! Everything changed. Hormones, it turns out, were the missing ingredients in the elusive chemical composition of *adventurous teen*.

The day they finally conceded, "Okay, maybe you did see a ghost", was the day I set my plan in motion.

Chapter One
A Fool Proof Plan

On that summer day in 1982, Kevin was the first of us to arrive at the Briarwood Mall. We normally spent our afternoons down at the local arcade, being too young for jobs and left mostly unsupervised. There we fed quarter after quarter from our allowances into the *Galaga*, *Frogger*, *Pac-Man*, or *Centipede* slots, and then went in on a shared giant Pepsi from the soda fountain with a large bag of Doritos. We never cared that we covered the control sticks in sticky orange nacho dust.

On the days we got bored with the arcade we would take the city bus down to the mall. There we could sit around for hours talking about everything and absolutely nothing. After that we would wander the music store to waste the remainder of the day browsing through albums most of us couldn't afford to buy.

I saw Kevin across the food court as he sat at a table closest to the window that looked out over the parking lot. The floor to ceiling windows were coated in something to keep the food court from becoming unbearably hot, yet still allowing enough natural light to make it welcoming. He was a tall guy with a big mess of dark brown hair, who dressed somewhat preppie. That day he wore a light blue Izod collared shirt, white tennis shorts, and his overworked leather boat shoes without socks.

He was busy playing with a new digital watch that had a calculator on it. He always had the newest gadgets, as was evident by the Radio Shack bag next to his foot. Being adopted into a wealthy family had its perks. Next to the other foot was a bag from Camelot Music filled with the newest releases on cassette.

MTV had debuted the year prior, and introduced our town to a whole new world of music, fashion, and culture. Until then, when an artist or band wanted to promote a new single they would show up on Solid Gold or American Bandstand and awkwardly lip sync to their hit song. The local radio normally played Billboard 100 stuff, or 70s Rock-n-Roll standards, but with MTV, a flood of cool bands coming out of Britain started to make the rotation. The "new wave" had arrived! When these bands began to infiltrate our music stores, it was a welcome breath of fresh air.

"Hey, Kev!" I said as I sat down across from him. Without asking I took a sip of his mystery soda, which turned out to be root beer that day, and swiped one of his french fries. I couldn't help grinning mischievously at the exasperated look on his face.

"You know, you could ask," he said, pretending to be disappointed in my lack of etiquette.

"Yeah, but where's the fun in that?" I joked, and took another fry. He swatted playfully at my hand.

Andrea showed up next. She had her brown hair in a ponytail, tied up with a yellow cotton scarf, and giant hoop earrings. Her bikini tan lines were in full display above her blue tube top with a ruffle across the front, which matched her white skirt and flats. She was obsessed with The Go-Go's and everything Los Angeles. That day she did her best to dress like she had just stepped out of the video for "Our Lips are Sealed".

I envied that she was always able to afford to keep up with whatever was the latest in fashion. Kevin and Andrea both came from families who were well off. To be fair though, anyone, in my opinion, who could afford to buy clothes when they wanted, or buy the albums when they came out, and not just wait for Christmas, were well off.

I felt a bit underwhelming in comparison, with a basic red striped t-shirt, belted light blue jean shorts, and my go-to white strap Bass sandals.

"Oh my god! I need fries now." She turned around and immediately b-lined for the Burger King window. She returned a few minutes later with a coke, a tray full of fries, and several overflowing cups of ketchup.

Third to arrive was Cat... her name was actually Catherine, but she had insisted on being called Cat ever since she was eight. She *was* obsessed with felines when she was really little, but I am not sure that is what prompted the insistence that no one was ever to call her Catherine again. I assumed it was the same reason I decided to go by "Gwen" - I hated my full name.

As she walked across the food court, Cat's short dark hair bobbed up and down with each step. A pair of baggy shorts displayed scrawny, pale legs above her black Converse high-tops. I teased her a lot about being part vampire, because as an artistic introvert, she didn't spend much time in the sun. Tucked into her shorts was a baggy Sex-Pistols concert t-shirt, probably one stolen from her older brother, Mike. It had a huge British flag splashed across the front with an image of the Queen in the center. Across her face, in cut out letters like a hostage note, was the song title: "God Save the Queen".

After a round of greetings, Cat immediately grabbed Kevin's bag of cassettes to see what new ones he had bought.

"Oh, Oingo Boingo!" she squealed. "I thought you already had this." She turned the *Only a Lad* cassette over in her hands to read the track listing. Then she noticed his fries, and proceeded to take one. Kevin wasn't bothered by that, so I tried to take another fry for myself, only to be met with him batting away my hand again.

"Seriously, guys! Get your own!" he chided, and then shoved the rest of them in his mouth at one time. "HA!" he blurted out through full cheeks.

Erin and Chris were the last to show up. Erin had to wait until her parents could drop her off. They were protective of her, and who she hung out with, so she had to really convince them to let her come that day. They didn't want her hanging out with kids who might be bad influences on their innocent little girl. What they didn't know was that, when she was away from them, she was anything but innocent.

In her tight pastel pink jeans, high wedge sandals, and ruffled white blouse, she sauntered up to our table. She tossed her wavy, long dirty-blonde hair over one shoulder, and the familiar smell of clove cigarettes wafted over us. She had probably lit up outside as soon as her parents had driven off.

"Hey guys!" she said, taking one of Andrea's fries and dipping it into the ketchup. She then proceeded to take off her modest blouse to reveal a tight spaghetti strap tank top. It had a giant heart across it, which demanded the attention of any passing boys. She glanced around hoping that she had caught the eye of one or two.

Cat and I exchanged a knowing look, and rolled our eyes at each other. "Nice heart," Cat managed to say with a straight face.

"I know, right?" Erin smiled, completely oblivious to Cat's sarcasm.

When Chris showed up, he waved a casual hello as he flipped his sandy brown bangs away from his eyes.

"Sorry I am late. I missed the first bus," he said as he walked up to our table. As he passed Erin he did a poor job of pretending to not notice her display of womanhood. He made eye contact with Cat and I for a second and was clearly embarrassed that we saw him noticing, which made him blush. He immediately maneuvered over to where Kevin was sitting to start talking music and movies. They usually spoke in movie quote language that would make no sense to anyone who had not seen what they were referencing. The rest of us were used to it though. We had all been friends since kindergarten.

Chris wasn't as tall as Kevin, but he'd definitely gotten taller since we graduated eighth grade. He loved his skateboard, which he carried with him everywhere, and he wore his usual scuffed Vans. A plaid flannel was tied around the waist of his 501 jeans, above which he sported his *Dark Side of the Moon* Pink Floyd concert t-shirt. His wardrobe didn't change very often, with the exception of a steady rotation of 70s classic rock concert t-shirts.

We kept our usual chit chat to a minimum that day because we had met up for a very specific reason, to work on a plan for my big birthday adventure the next day.

It wasn't much of a "plan" really, just a brainstorming of what to bring, initially only settling on the necessities: snacks. It took Kevin, the legitimate ex-Boy Scout, to remind us that we would be hiking all day and needed liquids as well as flashlights. Some of us argued that it was daylight, so why would we need flashlights? We girls discussed our outfits for the hike, while the boys debated on knives and matches as if they were going camping for a week... in bear country.

The girls were also not *into* wearing backpacks. At school we carried books and stuff in shoulder bags, or bags that hung from our arms, but never a backpack. So it was decided *for* the boys that they would have to be the ones carrying everything.

A big part of the plan had been to convince Cat's brother, Mike, to give us a ride. Where we were going was much too far to walk. She bartered with chores, which I offered to help her with, and he finally agreed.

I told my parents that I wanted to hang out with *just* my friends on the day of my birthday. They were fine with that, because my birthday fell mid-week, and they had to work. Instead, they had planned a special birthday dinner for me at Bennigan's the coming weekend. It was one of the few nice restaurants in town.

Andrea and Erin had already arranged to ride on the city bus home with me from the mall, and spend two nights. In their bags were overnight supplies as well as a change of clothes for hiking. Their parents were a lot stricter than mine, so they lied. They said we'd be doing a birthday picnic all day at the park, *but* that my parents would be there. We figured their parents would pick them up the following day from my house, and would never be the wiser.

We all agreed to meet up the next morning and walk over to Cat's house by 9:00 a.m. It seemed like a fool proof plan.

Chapter Two
Adventure Time

The following morning we got up early to my radio alarm clock, groggily ate some Frosted Flakes, dressed, and each of us doused ourselves with a healthy amount of Jean Nate. It had a refreshing citrus smell, like summer.

We walked down Trillium Drive past two houses, and turned the corner onto Rhododendron Way where Chris lived. We spotted him waiting out front. Aside from the color, a faded yellow, Chris and I lived in almost identical houses, single-story cracker boxes.

He was dressed in his usual skate boarder/surfer casual attire, with a Rolling Stones logo t-shirt on: a giant pair of red lips with a big red tongue sticking out. He smelled of Irish Spring, and his hair was wet as if he had just come straight from the shower. He also had his skateboard leaning up against his leg at the ready.

"Hey guys!" he called out as we walked across his dry lawn covered in dandelions.

"Hi," Erin said smiling cheerfully. Andrea gave a simple wave.

I pointed at his skateboard, as we came up even with him on the front stoop, "Dude, you can't bring that." Our casual familiarity with each other was due to being best friends and neighbors our whole lives.

"Oh, yeah... duh!" He opened up his front door and placed it against the hallway wall, making sure it didn't fall over.

"Can you put this in your pack for me?" I asked, after he'd shut the door behind him. I held out a large brown paper sack with our snacks and drinks for him to grab.

"Good morning to you too, Gwen," he said sarcastically. "Did someone wake up on the wrong side of the bed?"

"Yeah, I guess so. Sorry. I've been trying to pull this day off for a long time, so I suppose I didn't sleep well."

"We didn't either, because you kept talking all night," Andrea chided.

"To be fair, Andrea... you wouldn't stop talking either," Erin said.

"No, I get it. It's a big day." Chris knelt down over the opening of his pack, and tried to flatten the sack on top of his cheap knock-off Walkman in all its bright red and white plastic glory. There really wasn't much room for anything, due to his priority being exclusively cassette tapes.

"Did you even bring anything to eat or drink?" I asked, kneeling down beside him and sorting through his collection. "All I see is Foreigner... Led Zeppelin... The Doors... Cheap Trick and Styx."

Nodding, Chris replied confidently, "Pop-Tarts, and a bag of hotdogs!" His expression indicated that in his mind they were the most reasonable hiking food choices ever. "And what about you guys? Hmmm... let's see," he mocked while rummaging into our paper sack lunch, "Cheddar cheese sandwiches on white bread, little boxes of raisins, and carrot sticks. Are you still in sixth grade?" he teased.

"We were awesome sixth graders!" Andrea proudly countered.

"Remember sixth grade *camp*?" I blurted out. "You know what wasn't that awesome: the cafeteria fish sticks, and then puking later on our night hike!" I started cracking up when I saw the grimace on Erin's face as she visualized the memory – priceless.

"Ugh! Gross, Gwen!" Erin exclaimed trying to suppress a grin.

"Whatever. Let's book it," Chris ordered, as he threw his pack over one shoulder and started out.

We headed back to Trillium Drive, and then followed that up to Azalea Street, where we headed east for a quarter mile to Kevin's house. Off of Azalea, we came upon a giant brick wall with a plaque that read: Blackwood Estates. From there a drive led up a slight hill that ended in a cul-de-sac.

Every house on this drive looked like it should have been on the front of a magazine for the rich and famous. Most of the homes were at least two-stories, built from a combination of wood and brick, with tiered landscaping consisting of rock walls and ornate bushes trimmed in perfect symmetry. All the lawns were green with tidy borders of blooming flowers.

We walked up about three houses and saw him waiting for us in front of his sculpted oak front door. The relief was of an eagle soaring over a pine tree forest surrounding a lake. The eagle held a salmon in its talons. On either side of the beautiful door were long panes of stained glass with images of swamp reeds.

"I am *in love* with this door, Kevin! Can I just live here on the front porch?" I begged, only half joking. "I promise I won't bother anyone."

"I'll ask my mom next time I see her," he said as he hoisted up his oversized wilderness guide pack bursting full with everything but the kitchen sink.

We walked from his house back down Azalea to where it crossed Briarwood, the main avenue that connected all our neighborhoods, and headed south. After a few more minutes walk, we reached Kildeer Lane where Cat lived. Her neighborhood was older than all the rest - the houses looked like they had been built in the 1950s. Here the trees were more mature which gave the area more personality than Kevin's conservative cul-de-sac, but in exchange the houses were pretty run down and in need of upkeep.

She was waiting at her front door waving as we approached. When we joined her on the stoop, Erin was already complaining that it was time for a break. She sat down on the brick steps and pulled out a clove cigarette, lit up, and inhaled deeply.

"Oh my god, that is soooo much better. This has already been a looooong morning."

"Erin, we still have a long hike in front of us once we get there," Chris reminded her. He reached out his hand to take the cigarette that she was offering him, and he also took in a long drag. He noticed my disapproving stare out of the corner of his eye.

"What?" he asked, still trying to hold in his breath, then choked and laughed as he blew out the smoke.

"I guess it's a good thing my mom is already at work," Cat said. "Jeez!" She waved her hand to blow away the cloud of smoke collecting in front of her door.

Kevin offered to take Cat's supplies and put them into his backpack. He had to make room by getting out his Members Only windbreaker and tying it around his waist. It was mid-summer in southwestern Oregon, and the weather was supposed to be a perfect 85 degrees as an expected high, but Kevin's Boy Scout motto was "be prepared for anything".

With that in mind, we girls had at least traded in the previous day's sandals for tennis shoes, and were all wearing t-shirts and long jeans.

Once ready, we climbed into Mike's 1975 blue Oldsmobile *Starfire*. Its matching blue vinyl interior reeked of cigarettes. The dirty carpet stank of stale beer and was littered in empty cans. The backseat was only meant for two people comfortably, being that it was a hatchback, but Andrea, Erin, Chris and I had to find a way to cram in. We had Andrea sit across the top of us with her legs out, which allowed her no head room and forced her to hunch over. I could feel a spring from the seat poking up through the vinyl into my thigh. Kevin had to sit up in the front next to Mike, because of his long legs, and Cat, being the smallest, sat self-consciously on his lap.

Throughout the ride, we exchanged glances with each other over the overwhelming odor of Mike's B.O., but no one dared mention anything about it. We got to our destination about a half hour later, completely cramped, and everyone complaining about their legs falling asleep.

Mike pulled off the freeway onto the shoulder and came to a stop. The car idled loudly, while puffs of gray, oily smoke spewed out of the tailpipe. We clumsily stumbled our way out of the car, and the boys retrieved their packs. Mike leaned across the passenger seat out the open window and yelled: "I will be back here at 8 p.m.! You better be here! I am not going to just wait around. And remember, Cat, you owe me!" Cat obediently nodded back, and yelled, "thank you!"

With that, he peeled out in the gravel, trying to gain traction, and then pulled back onto the freeway. We were left choking on the smoke cloud he left behind. I looked down at my grandmother's gold-plated wrist-watch; it was 9:45 a.m. The watch was gifted to me on my 10th birthday, which just happened to be the last time that I had been back to that forest. I wound it up so I wouldn't lose the time later.

We stood side by side, with our gaze facing upward in contemplation of the long trek ahead. We must have been quite the sight to cars passing by, with our backs to the freeway as the heat radiated off of the cement in the warm mid-morning sun.

Looking up, I was struck with a moment of self-doubt. Up to that point, I had been so driven to make this day happen, but I found myself wondering, *what have I gotten us into*? I knew that we still had quite a climb ahead of us to get to the train tracks that circled around from the Douglas Zoo, and that it was even further up from there to get to our destination at the summit: the old Victorian house.

"Remind me again why we are doing this, Gwen?" Kevin asked, as he flipped his hair away from his brown eyes, and tightened down the shoulder straps of his heavy pack.

"We're looking for a ghost!" I replied.

Chapter Three
The Unprepared Expedition

As I started taking my first few steps into the knee high forest undergrowth the reality of why I was there started to really sink in. For the others, the day was just an exciting adventure, an alternative to summer boredom, but for me it was different. I began to feel anxious and was filled with worry.

What are we going to find if we actually can get inside the house? What had the boy been trying to tell me all those years ago? What if he turns out to be an angry spirit?

My thoughts were interrupted by Andrea, who was grumbling as she followed directly behind me, trying to walk in the footprints I left behind. I in turn was trying to put my feet into the spaces where Kevin stepped, but his stride was too long. At least his height was good for moving branches out of our way, because there was no natural path.

Climbing up the ravine from the freeway was not the way normal people entered the park, but there did not seem to be any other logical way to gain access. We knew we couldn't get off the train on the tracks, so we just decided to avoid the zoo and find our own way.

As Kevin hacked at the shrubs with a stick, like it was a machete, he boasted about his awesome survival skills. We still had yet to see if he could put any of that Boy Scout training to use, other than bullying his way through the undergrowth.

Beyond the sound of the stick breaking the bushes up in front of us, I noticed the sound of birds becoming more distinct. It stood out because the constant white-noise of the city had fallen away, and there was a noticeable absence of car sounds.

Cat walked behind Andrea, followed by Erin, with Chris taking up the rear. I overheard him talking to the girls as we made our way up.

"I'll stay behind, to, you know, keep an eye out for danger," he said trying to sound gallant. "Someone has to keep you *laaay-deees* safe!"

"Yeah, right!" Erin said, tossing her hair flirtatiously. "So, how's the view from back there?"

"I'm sorry I can't hear you!" he smirked as he pointed to his headphones, and clicked play.

Cat was being her usual quiet self. Once her brother, Mike, had been out of sight, she took off the oversized sweatshirt she was wearing, to show off yet another band t-shirt that she swiped from his closet. This time it was The Ramones. The image was of the band standing around in front of a building with the song title "Sheena is a Punk Rocker" spray painted on a wall like graffiti.

When she tied the sweatshirt around her waist, she looked even skinnier than normal. She hadn't "blossomed" quite like the rest of us had, and I noticed she was becoming more and more uncomfortable around Andrea and Erin. Those two gossiped all the time about everyone, they were boy crazy, *and* they were trying out to be cheerleaders - a combination that sometimes could be insufferable. It was a totally different world than the one Cat lived in. Even though they'd gone to school together their whole lives, and Cat's older brother Mike was friends with Erin and Andrea's older sisters, they were slowly growing apart.

The older sisters, being seventeen, had a lot of influence over what we were exposed to, such as the newest music, which was *not* being played on Casey Kasem's *Top 40 Coast-to-Coast*. Erin's sister had turned us on to The Police. I became obsessed, and listened to the entire *Ghost in the Machine* album over and over.

They also helped ease us into puberty, understand our bodies, and how to navigate our boy crushes. Cat didn't have that, so she was uncomfortable with anything other than guy things. I walked a unique road between those worlds: comfortable as a tomboy, yet able to be lost in artistic endeavors for hours, while also enjoying a good sleepover with girly things and gossip.

We continued to climb, but as it got steeper, it became increasingly more difficult. The canopy of trees was closing in above, and only small patches of sunlight escaped through. The ground that had looked solid from the road was actually spongy due to the thick layers of old pine needles, dead plants, and ivy. The plethora of ivy was crazy! It grew everywhere. The vines wound through the ferns on the ground, and twisted up each tree, completely choking them out. In some places it looked like the only thing keeping the rotten, moss-covered trees standing were the mass of vines.

In order to keep moving forward, I had to bring my leg up nearly to my chest just to lift it over the crowded foliage and fallen tree branches. It was tedious. Our thighs burned, and any part of our bodies that were not covered up were being scratched or eaten by bugs.

Kevin took no notice of the four of us in the middle of the pack, constantly complaining, and exclaiming "crap" every two seconds. He didn't even notice when at one point we all sat down in protest. Chris called out, but Kevin didn't hear him. He had to chuck dirt clods up the path to hit him in the arm or leg to get him to turn around. That's when we realized he'd donned his Walkman. Kevin was lost in his own world.

When he took the headphones off and turned to us, Andrea called out, "Hey, space cadet! Like, whatcha listening to?"

He pulled out a yellow plastic case that read Men at Work, and held it up like a new father. "Who Can it Be Now?" he announced.

"I don't know... who *can* it be?" Cat asked trying to keep a straight face.

"Ha. Ha. Very funny," Kevin said unwilling to give her the satisfaction of breaking a straight face.

"Aw, man that's rad!" Andrea exclaimed. "Can we take turns listening to it?"

"Chris will give you one of his Pop-Tarts, if you let us!" I offered beguilingly.

Chris, hearing his name, countered with, "Hey, leave my Pop-Tarts out of this. Those are mine. Give him one of your lame carrots!"

"You had to mention food. Now I am hungry," Cat scolded. "I brought a box of Cheese-Its! Kevin, pass those down."

Kevin flung off his pack and squatted down. He dug out the box, passed it to me, and I handed it down the line.

"Chris can you give us our juice boxes?" I asked. Chris also squatted down and unzipped his pack. He took out the only three containers there were and tossed one to each of us.

"Is that all you guys brought?" Chris asked, searching through the paper sack with our stuff.

"Yeah, we couldn't scrounge up much more than that. I had hoped it would last us longer," I responded. Looking at Cat, I said, "Sorry I didn't have more."

Cat nodded with a mouth full of Cheese-Its, that it was okay. She untied her sweatshirt to show us an olive drab canvas covered canteen strapped around her waist on an army belt, apparently from her dad's belongings. He'd been in the Vietnam War when she was a baby.

Kevin patted his two thermoses on either side of his pack. Chris said he had a couple cans of Pepsi that apparently had been hiding under his pile of tapes. This rally of resources gave us a mental boost and further confidence that we wouldn't wither away in an afternoon.

"Mmmmm, it smells soooo good," I said aloud, as I closed my eyes for a second and inhaled deeply. The air was filled with wonderful aromas: rich soil, dried pine needles, old wood, wild flower blooms, and freshly fallen oak leaves.

Cat closed her eyes and inhaled, while simultaneously munching on her last handful of Cheese-Its. She coughed, and struggled not to choke, then finally had to spit everything out as she gasped for air. Kevin and Chris, in their extreme worry for her well being, cracked up, which only made her cough more as tears streamed down her face.

"I'm sorry for making you smell the forest," I apologized, as I tapped my hand on her back. Andrea and Erin started chuckling, as Cat continued to recover.

"Do you hear that?" Kevin asked, as he looked down at his watch. "Shhh... listen."

We sat quietly and could hear the sound of the train going by somewhere in the hills above us. In an instant the sound triggered the memory of leaning out the window of the passenger car pointing at the boy in the forest, trying to get the people around me to see him. I could see him clear as any one of them, and yet no one else could.

"You okay, Gwen?" Cat asked, touching my arm gently.

"Oh, yeah. Just remembering something, that's all. We really should get going." I stood up, wiped the dirt from my Bill Blass jeans, and slipped into my new white OP windbreaker that had a rainbow across the chest; *actual* brand-name birthday gifts from my grandparents.

The windbreaker had been tied around my waist since that morning, but the lack of sunlight under the dense canopy had made it quite chilly. Chris took the opportunity to put on his red plaid flannel that had been tied around his waist as well. Erin and Andrea grumbled with jealousy. They only had on thin striped t-shirts tucked into their designer jeans.

Kevin glared at them with that look like, "I told you so." In response they rolled their eyes and growled in unison.

"We know. We know…'always be prepared'!" Andrea replied dismissively.

Kevin raised his eyebrows, crossed his arms and glanced back and forth between the two girls.

After a moment of silence, like a spaghetti western standoff, Erin complained, "Oh my god, we get it Kevin! But it's supposed to be like a million degrees today."

"Not in here," he countered, gesturing his hand around at the surroundings.

"How were we supposed to know that?" Andrea asked, rolling her eyes at him, and then looking at me in disappointment. I shrugged, feigning ignorance.

Falling back in step behind Kevin, we continued lumbering up the hill through the undergrowth. Chris followed up the rear of the pack putting his headphones back on, and then he quietly hummed along to the haunting melody of "Riders on the Storm".

Chapter Four
The Embankment

After another grueling half hour of navigating our way up the center of the ever steepening ravine, we reached the slippery gravel base of what looked like a man-made embankment. It stood like a tall wall in front of us made out of dirt and rubble rock, with nature trying to take root where it could. Random shrubs and tree saplings stuck out here and there. The ivy surrounding the ravine had, over time, crept its way across the area to grab hold as well.

The embankment curved inward following the natural arc cut out of the hillside that was part of the ravine. It dawned on me that I was standing in the same "horseshoe" area where I used to look down from the train and imagine falling over and being left stranded.

A chill ran up my spine. I spun around surveying the forest around us, convinced someone was there watching us. I thought for sure I would see that boy peek around a tree, or peer out from the shadows of the tall ferns, but no one was there. I was being overwhelmed with feelings again of being afraid, and sad.

"Is everything okay?" Cat asked with genuine concern. "You keep doing that thing."

"What thing?" I asked, still looking around.

"Do you see him?" she whispered, looking around as well.

Cat had been the only one of all of them who had believed my story from the beginning. We never told the others, but Cat had her own ghost experience - her dad. She insisted that she could see him sometimes in her house, even though he had been dead for five years. She told me she wasn't afraid of him, she always knew he was just there to look out for her, and it made her feel comforted. When alone in her room, she would talk with him and tell him about her day.

I leaned in towards her, "No, but I do feel like we're being watched. I am having all these strange... feelings. It reminds me of that day I saw him. I wonder if what I am experiencing are *his* feelings."

"What do you mean?" she asked.

"Lonely, helpless, lost... I don't really feel that way, ya know?"

"Hmmm..." she pondered. "Well, that is why we are here today, to figure this out, right? If he is lost we will help him find his way out."

"Right. You are sounding like a character right out of *Ghost Story*!" I teased. "I should have known better than to loan my book to you."

"You didn't. I saw it at the theater with Mike," Cat boasted.

"But that was rated R! How did you get in?" I asked.

"What are you guys talking about?" Andrea asked, as she and Erin walked up. They stood there staring up at the top of the embankment and watched as Chris and Kevin tried to figure out a way up.

"Movies," I answered quickly to divert away from the actual subject matter.

"Mike turned seventeen last August. He just showed his I.D. and he was able to get my ticket." She shrugged like it was no big deal. I had forgotten that even though Mike and the sisters were going into their senior year, he was older than the rest of them. Held back in kindergarten, he would be eighteen the entire senior year.

"Oh you are so lucky!" Erin said. "That sure beats trying to sneak in all the time."

"The train runs every 40 minutes," Kevin said out loud to remind us. "We'll need to hide when it comes back by. So we better figure this out fast."

Chris walked along the base searching for a good path up, slipping every now and then on a loose section of rock. The ivy that had taken over some parts of the embankment seemed promising, and he groped about until he found a hand hold that was sturdy enough to use as a rope. He started climbing up, but without tread on his Vans he slipped constantly, and had to use mostly his upper body strength to pull himself up.

Once there, he told us to follow the same path. Andrea tried, but the vine gave way, causing her to slide backwards. Had she been all the way up when it happened it would have been about a ten foot fall - nothing deadly, but it definitely would have hurt. Chris pointed out an alternate vine, and she tried that, but couldn't get a foot hold in the loose rock.

"Here, let me help. Okay, put your foot on my knee, and then pull yourself up with your arms. Chris, grab her and pull her up!" Kevin said, as they, together, assisted Andrea's assent.

"Remember when he rented *The Shining* for us?" Cat continued. "My mom would never have let us watch that."

"Yeah," I replied as I watched Andrea's progress.

"Redrum…" Cat whispered in a creepy voice.

"You enjoy doing that, don't you?" I asked, pushing at her shoulder playfully.

"Doing what?" Cat feigned innocence, then chuckled menacingly as we walked over towards Kevin for our turn.

Once Andrea had climbed all the way up, he used the same method for Erin, and then once she'd made it, Chris called out to me, "Gwen, come on. It's not that hard."

Never being one to pass on a challenge Chris handed down, I used Kevin's knee to step up, found a foothold with my other foot on the root of a shrub sticking out, and pulled myself up the vine like a rope. I made it up without too much struggle, as

Chris tugged under my shoulders to help me climb up onto the tracks.

Cat, on the other hand, had no upper body strength, so Kevin, all too willingly, put his arms around her and then lifted her halfway up the entire section. He then had her rest her feet in his hands as she reached up to Chris and I to pull her the rest of the way. I noticed her blushing.

"Do you like Kevin?" I mouthed silently as I was pulling her up to the tracks. She turned her face away, acting like she didn't see what I was asking.

Kevin, who had been our fearless leader up to that point, could not find any branches or vines that would hold his weight. Although not fat, he was just a big guy. He also could not find a foothold, because his feet were too large for any of the outcroppings of vegetation. We watched on, feeling his frustration, as attempt after attempt failed. Suddenly Chris yelled out for everyone to hide… he could hear the train coming.

We frantically started looking around for a place to hide, knowing that once the train came around the bend to curve inward we would be visible to all the passengers.

Cat panicked and started scurrying back down the vine, jumping into Kevin's arms. They managed to flatten themselves against the embankment wall to remain undetected.

Chris grabbed my hand and pulled me across the tracks towards the cliff face. Instead of climbing however, he dug into the bushes and ivy vines, like a badger. I realized what he was trying to do and started helping. I called out to Erin and Andrea, who were frozen in indecision, "Over here! Hurry!"

They snapped out of it and ran over, but Erin caught her toe on the edge of the last track and tumbled into the soft foliage.

Andrea helped her up. "Are you okay? You totally almost ate it."

"Yeah, yeah," she breathed heavily, and continued to hurry over to the hollow Chris and I had made. I tucked in as far as I could go, and pulled my legs up to my chest. Wrapping my arms around my shins, I tried to make myself as small as possible. Chris curled in after me, facing into my side, with Andrea pushing on his back for him to squish in further.

"Move! Move! Move!" she whispered to him, nearly panicking. Erin in turn pushed on Andrea's back saying the same thing, with the addition of, "Oh my god! Oh my god! Oh my god!"

"Erin, stop freaking out!" Andrea scolded.

Once all four of us where crammed into the hollow, we pulled the vines and branches back over us like shutting a door.

Chris' face was smooshed up next to mine. "Funny meeting you here," he quipped.

"Oh, stop it," I smirked.

Andrea said, "I have to pee." This made Erin snort, and she covered her mouth to try to not laugh out loud. Tears started streaming down Andrea's face as it contorted in suppressed laughter. "Stop it,

Erin. I'm serious!" That only made the laughing more difficult to muffle.

I did my best to hold in the nervous giggles threatening to rise. I was distracted, however, by the realization that my finger was being stroked. Chris' arm had come around the front of me, part of making room for the girls, where his hand came to rest on mine. The sensation made me hyper aware of the heat of his breath on my cheek.

What has gotten into him? I thought to myself. *Does he mean to be doing that?*

As the train passed by, each car a din of loud adults speaking and children laughing, dust and gravel kicked up all around us. I stifled a cough as I turned to look at him. He stared back at me not averting his gaze. He had light brown eyes. I'd always known they were that color, I think. I am not sure why the depth of that brown was suddenly so fascinating. It was like I had never *really* looked into anyone's eyes until then.

All at once he wasn't that little kid I played Nerf football with, or went on day long bike rides with, or stood in line for hours with to see Star Wars. He was a cute... boy... dude. Had he always been that attractive? If he had, I only just noticed.

The rhythmic thumping of the train passing was drowned out by the loud beat of my heart and the swooshing sound in my ears from blood pumping so quickly through my veins. I got light- headed. I think he knew. Maybe I was blushing, I don't know, but he smiled.

Chapter Five
Destination Summit

Andrea and Erin scrambled out of the hollow back up onto the tracks, while Chris slowly scooted back away from me, not averting his eyes, and allowing his hand to linger on mine. He was obviously gauging the way I would react, and by the smile, I think he was pleased. I was surprised in myself, quite frankly. The rush of feelings towards him came out of left field.

5

The previous school year, eighth grade, I had been going steady with a guy named Ryan. Going on a date meant hang outs at the mall, or the arcade, or at other people's houses when parents were away. Andrea had been going steady with Ryan's best friend, Jonathan. Erin had a crush on a guy named Jacob, but the crush had gone unrequited until the dance at the end of the year. The dance was the first time we were able to put on dresses, be dropped off at school after hours, and dance with our boyfriends.

We had felt so grown up, despite being thirteen or fourteen. At one point, Andrea and I completely freaked out seeing Erin and Jacob making out on the dance floor, slow dancing to Air Supply. When she came up to breathe, and saw us staring at her, she almost died of embarrassment. We were mouthing to her, "Right on!" with a 'thumbs up' approval. She turned crimson red and buried her head against Jacob's shoulder.

After graduation, during summer vacation, Ryan and Jonathan started training to try out for the high school football team, and I guess newer babes were in their sights. We got break up calls over the phone. Ryan called Andrea on behalf of Jonathan, and Jonathan called me on behalf of Ryan. It was humiliating. It was devastating. It felt like the universe had crushed me, and life would end as I knew it.

Ryan had been my first love; what I thought was the "real thing". He had been everything to me that spring. Two months... a lifetime! Puberty, I suppose, is weird that way: everything is exaggerated and overwhelming.

Chris had tried to console me during our hours-long conversations on the phone. This followed previous hours-long conversations with Erin and Andrea and Cat. An expression my father used often that year was, "Gwen! Stop monopolizing the phone!"

The usual response was, "Okay, Okay... I'll get off in just a minute."

An hour later, he'd be yelling again.

5

Chris offered his hand to help me stand up once I crawled out of the space, and he held it longer than usual, again seeing how I would react. I remember looking around nervously at everyone else standing on the tracks. I saw Erin staring at us, and immediately dropped my hand away. I could see the hurt in his eyes. I don't know why I responded that way. It just made me nervous, and giggly, and sweaty, and totally self conscious. Pretending it hadn't happened seemed like the logical course to follow.

"Where's Cat?" I asked the girls, trying to avert attention from myself.

"Umm… down here!" I heard Cat call out. Her voice sounded really strange. We walked over to the embankment ledge and peered down. Kevin had Cat in his arms again and was pushing her up to grab hold of a vine. Andrea put her hand down for her to grab once she got high enough. Cat's face was unnaturally red. She caught my eye, and instantly looked away. I don't know how I knew, but I knew. Chris caught on as well.

"Sooooo… Kev. My main man. What's shaking?" He tugged as hard as he could on Kevin's hand, walking backwards to help him scramble up, and then he looked over at Cat, grinning.

Cat hit Chris on the arm, and playfully scorned him, "Dream on!"

"Me, dream on? Uh, duh, it's so obvious." Chris looked to Kevin for some sort of confirmation.

Kevin, instead kept a straight face and turned to look up the hill, "Let's get truckin'," he said and then immediately cut across the tracks and started climbing the last section of hill to reach the summit. "We are going to need to do this quickly before the train comes back by."

With a new sense of urgency, we shook ourselves out of the romantic yearnings of hormonal youth, and started scrambling up the last shorter, yet steeper slope.

Erin kept slipping because her brown suede Puma sneakers had no tread. "Craaaap!" she yelled as she slid back down to where she'd started.

"Why did you wear those anyways?" I asked. "They're totally worn out from P.E."

"The yellow stripe matched my shirt," she responded.

Chris sarcastically muttered, "Can't argue with that logic!"

After another slip and a branch nearly ripping the calf of her jeans, she yelled "This is soooo bogus! Gwen, this better be worth it. I am like, so over alllllll of this."

"No one said you *had* to come! You wanted to," I reminded her. "Come on, we're almost to the top! We can do this."

"Why didn't Jacob come with us?"Andrea asked Erin out of nowhere.

"I don't want to talk about him. He's a jerk, remember, Erin grumbled. "God, I wish I had stayed home."

Trying my best to lighten the mood, I started singing "Look at what's happened…"

"Gwen, don't even think about it," Cat complained, as I continued to sing.

"I love that show," Andrea countered.

"Nooooo!" Kevin protested loudly, pulling his headphones back on.

"Please kill me now," Chris pleaded, also doing the same.

In moments of tension, some people get quiet, but I was the annoying one who always broke into song. However, despite all the protesting, the girls couldn't help themselves and joined in.

We gave that last dozen feet our best final effort and soon found ourselves crawling up onto the summit into the midday heat. Andrea and Erin were thrilled to be back in the sun, and like lizards stretched their tan arms out to get all the warmth they could. Chris pretended to not look as they stretched, as he and I tied our jackets back around our waists.

Once we had a chance to take in the surroundings, I noticed that across the summit was a low wooden fence. It ran horizontally along a frontage road. On the opposite side of the road were parking spaces for a public park.

"Noooo way!" I exclaimed in disbelief. Everyone turned to see what I was staring at.

"Did you guys know that was there this whole time?" Erin asked in total disgust.

"I haven't been to the zoo in years; I had no idea," Andrea responded.

"Me either," I sighed. I never heard of a public park being built. "How does anyone even get up here? Where does that road go?"

"No clue," Chris said.

"I can't believe this…" Cat shook her head, "We could have just had Mike drop us off here."

Kevin was quiet for a moment, then concluded," Shiiiit… if this is a public park, that means there could be a parking lot attendant, or some sort of security."

"You mean security, like cops?" Erin asked.

"Yeah, so why don't we go over there towards the trees, just to be on the safe side. No one should be able to see us from there," Kevin suggested.

"Cops," I looked at Erin, giggling, "like Kojak. You know, 'bang bang'!"

Erin responded, "Oh…Kojak", putting on her best Japanese accent, "bang bang!" she finally smiled and laughed a little.

"Oh my god, that is one of my favorite movies!" Andrea declared.

"You may not want to admit it, but you know "Ready to Take a Chance Again" was your favorite song for a long time," I said.

"I won't admit it," she giggled in response.

As we all followed along behind Kevin towards a cluster of trees, Chris looked at us all like we'd all lost our minds.

"*Foul Play*! You know… with Chevy Chase," I explained. "There was that scene when they stole the taxi…" He stared at me blankly. "There were Japanese tourists in the back…" Giving up, I shook my head in exasperation.

"Psych!" Chris exclaimed. "I was just messing with you. Of course I know what you are talking about… duh!"

"Dudley Moore played a great sleaze bag in that movie," Kevin interjected out of nowhere. "He does the best drunk guy impression… like in *Arthur*." He then acted like he was intoxicated, and bumped into a bush. Slurring his words, he said, "Excuse me… oh, you're a hedge!" He then made himself stumble and fall over onto the ground.

Laughing, we all joined him on a grassy area out of view, sprawling out to take in the sun. Chris popped open a can of warm Pepsi and after taking a sip, passed it around.

"Remember Mrs. Shaw's English class, Andrea? When we were convinced she had a flask in her drawer 'cause she always seemed drunk?" I asked, turning to get her attention.

"And the way her eye always twitched when she got mad because we were passing notes in class!" Andrea started twitching her eye lid and pulling her face to look like a stroke victim. This started the fits of giggles all over again; with us rolling around on our backs like turtles, unable to turn over. Once these fits started it was hard to turn them off, because everything became funny. I think it was the hardest I had laughed in my whole life.

After a while, I managed to sit up to wipe the tears from my face and massage my cheek muscles. That is when I noticed a cone-shaped roof, poking up above tree line further down the clearing. "There it is!" I pointed, showing everyone where to look.

We'd come up the hill from the back side. When the train went around the bend leaving the cut out section, it headed in that direction. This would have been the point where the house was visible to the passengers.

We walked along the edge of the summit towards a thicker grove of trees, and gradually the tall dilapidated Victorian house came into view. The cone shaped roof sat atop a tower centered between two gabled wings of the house. The tower itself looked like it had three main levels, with each wing of the house having two.

"Oh thank god!" Andrea declared. "If it had looked like the *Amityville Horror* house I would have died!"

"Now you are making me think of those glowing pig eyes," Erin shivered.

Kevin slowly snuck up from behind the two of them, poked each in the center of their backs and yelled, "Boo!" They leaped out of their skin, then immediately swung around to hit him.

"Agh, chill out. Chill out!" he cried out as he ran away laughing.

"KEVIN! Oh, my *god*! What is *wrong* with you?" Erin screamed after him. "Sooo not cool!" She shook furiously, taking in deep breaths.

"Shh! Jesus, Erin, be quiet!" Chris reminder her, "You don't want us to get caught do you?"

"Hey, he started it," she whispered loudly, as she glared at Kevin.

Andrea bent over with her legs crossed, "Okay, now I *really* have to pee." We started laughing all over again, trying to be quiet, as she ran off to find the privacy of a bush. "Don't look!"

Chapter Six
The House

The tower side faced kitty corner to us, looking out over the side of the summit that was visible to the train passing below. We could just see the cone of the tower looking like a witch's hat, peeking above the roof line.

The foundation had disintegrated in several areas, the brickwork crumbled to dust, leaving the whole house slightly tilted. In some places, where much of the brick foundation was missing, the beams meant to support the floor sagged precariously.

As we rounded the backside of the house we came upon a square, single-story gabled extension. This side of the house had been permanently shaded by trees. The whole roof on this side was completely covered in moss, and in places it had rotted and fallen in. The fascia still had a hint of its former teal green paint. The siding on the house was made up of narrow cedar clapboards, aged to a graying brown, running horizontally across each section. As with the roof above, here also were missing areas, where pieces had just fallen off or rotted away.

Midway up the wall were rectangular paired windows, surrounded by decorative casings, with segmented glass panes – one upper, one lower. It looked like the bottom pane lifted upwards, but none of the windows we tried budged. They were either nailed shut from the inside, or exposure to moisture and sun had caused the casement to swell.

"We should split up," Kevin suggested.

"Why?" I asked.

"That way we'll find a way in faster," he responded.

"Okay, whatever," Chris replied, as we then separated into two groups to search in opposite directions for a door or an open window.

We were avoiding the front porch with the main door, because that faced towards the park. We just hoped that being mid-week, there wouldn't be anyone around. We were wrong. A car motor could be heard cruising through every so often, followed by bouts of yelling from kids and their parents. These were definite signs that a parking lot attendant or a random parent might notice a group of kids trying to gain access to the house.

Technically we were trespassing. That really hadn't occurred to us until that moment. The house was fenced off from the park in such a way that indicated it was off limits, and we were going to have to break in if we wanted to explore.

Andrea seemed the most concerned by this realization. "Oh, man, my parents are going to kill me if they find out we are breaking in. I thought we were just exploring an old abandoned house. You said it was abandoned. Like, as if, like, no one cared!"

"I didn't know," I replied defensively. "I just wanted to come see what this place was all about and try to find some clues or something."

"Like the *Hardy Boys*!" Chris interjected sarcastically. He returned my glare, and shrugged innocently. "What?"

"No… like *Nancy Drew*!" Cat responded in my defense.

"They're both lame!" Kevin kidded. "*Bobbsey Twins* rule!

"Who the heck are the *Bobbsey Twins*?" Erin asked.

"Never mind," Kevin sighed. "Come on, let's find a way in. You guys go that way." He pointed in the opposite direction than he was headed.

Andrea, Chris and I went around the corner of the house, to find yet another single story addition, jutting out from the house. It was narrower though, with a flat roof. It was different than the rest of the architecture, something that might have been added later on. We tried the windows on each section; they wouldn't budge either.

Chris took his pack off, backed up, and looked up to the second story of the main house. There was another gabled roof, this one with elaborately carved bargeboards, projecting out over a section decorated in shingles that reminded me of fish scales. Beneath, there were two windows spaced a couple feet apart, overlooking the flat roof of the bottom extension. One had a wooden board in place of missing glass. The second window had a slight crack on the corner of its bottom pane, but was still intact. "I think I can get up there. Gwen put out your hands," he said.

He interlaced my fingers together, palm up, like a cradle, and then held his hands on mine for a second. We made eye contact.

"Guys... flirt later... let's get inside before somebody sees us," Andrea whispered loudly.

Chris blushed, and looked back at my hands, "I'll put my foot there, and you just shove me up. Once I can reach the roof I'll pull myself the rest of the way." I nodded okay. I had seen him do crazy stunts before and pull them off.

"No sweat!" he added, reassuring the both of us.

"Dude, you will never make it!" Andrea balked. She was pretending to be cool, but the shakiness in her voice gave away that she was losing her nerve the longer we stood exposed outside the house. Perhaps she hoped we would come to our senses and just turn back.

"Andrea, take a chill pill," he quipped.

"Bite me!" Andrea huffed, crossed her arms and turned away.

"You guys... lay off!" I chided, as I hoisted Chris up enough to grab hold of the roof's edge. He struggled to pull himself up, his feet scrambling against the clapboard panels, breaking a couple loose.

"Oh, crap," I whispered loudly, putting a finger to my lips. "Shhh." Finally he was able to swing a leg up for extra leverage and roll over onto the roof.

"*That* was gnarly!" Chris whispered back, as he sat up and leaned over to wave to us that everything was fine.

"Now it's your turn," he said as he waved at her to come up.

Andrea looked up at him in shock, "Me? No way, dude! You're stoned!"

"I haven't blazed all week," he smiled. "Okay, okay! No need to spaz out!"

"Just break in already and open a door or something!" Kevin quietly called out as he came back around the corner.

"I will! Check ya later!" He did a lame attempt at an actual salute, and then disappeared from view.

"Was there anything that way?" I asked as they came along side of us.

"Nope," Kevin responded.

"Where's Chris gone?" Erin asked, looking around expectantly.

"Did he find a way in?" Cat asked with excitement.

Andrea pointed to the roof, "He's up there." We heard the sound of glass breaking, and Chris cussing.

We all held still, and listened for any signs that the loud noise had brought unwanted attention our way. After a moment or two of only hearing the kids playing off in the distance, Kevin whispered upwards to Chris, "Smooth move Ex-Lax!"

Cat casually suggested, "I think we should have lunch when we get inside."

"Do you have a bottomless stomach or something?" Erin asked. "You're always hungry."

There was a tap at the downstairs window in front of us. Chris put his face up on the glass pane, smooshing his face against it. Using his lips he made a seal and blew, making his cheeks puff out.

I knocked on the window where his mouth was. "Just let us in!"

He backed off, and stood there grinning. Scrutinizing the inside window frame, he looked to see if there was any weakness in its defense against trespassers. He then turned around and left the room. Kevin leaned over the fading white painted window trim, to see where he had gone. The rest of us stood on our tip-toes trying to see in as well. The paint curled up in paper strips, like it had been shredded with a potato peeler.

"Here! Over this way," we heard him call out from where we had begun our search.

Hurrying back around the corner, under the shade of the trees, we found Chris with his head leaning out from one of the paired windows. "The nails were barely hanging on to anything in here," he said, "the wood just broke away as soon as I tugged on one. Come on." He waved us in with his hands.

"Why didn't you just open a door?" Kevin asked.

"I didn't see any. I mean, except the front one. Kind of thought we were avoiding the whole front of the house thing," he quipped.

"Here...let me lift each of you up," he offered as he extended his hands. With the exception of Kevin, the bottom of the window sill was at the same height as our heads.

With a boost from Kevin, Erin managed to reach Chris' outstretched hands. From inside, he pulled her over the sill. The wood crumbled a little as she made her way in.

"Thank you, Chris." I heard her coo once she was inside.

Next Kevin helped Andrea, but it took some coaxing from Cat and I. "It'll be okay. We won't get caught," I assured her. "I will be right behind you."

Kevin then grabbed me around the waist, and he said, "Jump on the count of three. One... two... three!" Up I went off the ground, as he lifted, aiming me toward the open window. I came down on my ribs, kind of hard, in the center of the window sill, half way in and half way out. Chris was there smiling, with his arms outstretched to pull me in.

He put his hands under my arms, pulled back on my torso, and lifted me up and into the room. As my feet touched the ground we found ourselves arm in arm, facing each other... lingering.

I heard Andrea cough subtly, and Erin groan. I could feel the flush rising to my nose and cheeks. My chest felt warm. We slowly dropped our arms, and our fingers touched for a few long seconds.

The moment was broken by Cat squirming in the window, stuck half in and half out, calling out for someone to help.

Chris broke away from me and walked towards her. He lifted her up and pulled her into the room until she was on her feet.

"Do *you* need help, Kev?" Chris called out.

"Nah, man, I got it," Kevin responded, throwing his pack in first, followed by Chris'. When each pack hit the decomposing wood flooring covered in layers of dust, billows of particles flew up into the air, causing all of us to choke and cough.

The undeniable foul musty smell of dirt and dampness from black mold was overpowering. The atmosphere was stagnant. Without flowing air, the space felt sickeningly warm. I set out immediately to see if I could find another window to open hoping to create a cross breeze. It felt like there was just not enough oxygen, even though I knew there was.

Crossing to the second window, I noticed how unstable the flooring was. With every step the boards would sink a little. The girls and I were pretty light, I was sure we would be fine, but Chris and Kevin could break through. Maybe even sprain and ankle or worse. "Be careful over here, you guys," I cautioned.

Along the walls were old rotted cupboards, doors hanging on rusted hinges. One corner, against the exterior wall, had a pipe hanging from the ceiling. There were soot marks against the wall ending down at a concrete slab, which I supposed had been for a wood stove to cook on. Another corner cupboard had a counter which had a metal basin built into it. There was no sign of any plumbing. Next to the cupboard was a large hole in the floor with a cover over it. "I wonder what this was used for," I asked aloud to no one in particular.

"Ewww... I hope that isn't like a toilet? This isn't an outhouse, is it?" Erin asked looking around.

At the window, I found what Chris had said was true. The wood was so rotted in this back room that one tug on the nails, and they came away with ease. I tried to lift the window, but it was stuck. "Erin. Andrea. Come here. Help me lift this."

Once all three of us pushed up against the resistance, it broke free and slid up quickly, letting free thousands of dead insects in the window jamb.

"OH MY GOD!" Erin screamed. She jumped back, swatting at invisible bugs that might have gotten on her, as she jumped up and down, turning in circles. "GROSS ME OUT!"

"There is nothing on you!" Cat laughed.

"Okay, this is really creeping me out! There are some still alive!" Andrea said with a slight bit of panic, peering into the crevices of the frame. She then squealed and ran over to Erin, both of them staying as far away as they could from the window.

I stood back as well, watching the bugs fall out all over the sill. They were only little pill bugs and earwigs, I noted. Still, the sight of them spilling out all over the place gave me the heebie jeebies, and I quickly hopped away to stand with the other cowards. Kevin walked over and pretended to pick one up and eat it, offering one to Chris. This caused us to squeal even more, cuss and make fake puking sounds.

"Nah, dude. I'm good," he laughed.

Chapter Seven
First Floor

After a thorough inspection of the decrepit back room, and settling down from having just broken in, we moved into a dark hallway.

A faint light filtered into the dark space from the right at the end of the hall. There, daylight illuminated from an entrance into a room. To the left, at the other end of the hallway, there was a door, hanging off its hinges that opened towards a set of stairs descending down into pure blackness.

"Nooooo way am I going down *there*!" Erin proclaimed. No one argued with her and, as a collective, we moved in the opposite direction.

At the end of the hall we turned left into a large open space. In the center of the room, where a chandelier or some other ornate light fixture once hung, exposed naked wires reached down through a hole like living tendrils. There were scorch marks around the hole, as if there had been a small fire. The flooring was made up of wood tiles in contrasting stains, creating a subtle checkerboard pattern. In the dead center of the floor, the stain was less worn. It had a shape of what might have been a large area rug; most likely where the dining room table had sat. The outer border, however, was scratched, and most the stain had worn away from foot traffic.

The room was completely devoid of furnishings. The only reminder of its former life was preserved within rectangles on the interior walls where family portraits or art once hung. Here you could still see details of the faded wallpaper's intricate design.

Cat and I were immediately drawn to those sections, looking closely at the design of Carnations, wheat sheaves, clam shells and doves all mixed in. The clam shell stood in the center, leaves and wheat sheaves branching out from all around it, a bouquet of Dahlias adorning it from below. On either side were mirror images of doves with either their wings outstretched over blooming flowers, or the plant leaves wrapping around the doves like a wreath. The colors might have been a pink blush against a blue background, but it was hard to tell because they had all faded to variations of brown and beige.

Also present on the walls were a few round holes, suggesting there might have been lighting sconces mounted. Within the holes we could see into the bones of the house, which were nothing but dust and cobwebs between wood framing.

Peering into the hole, Cat said, "I was hoping to find a hidden treasure map!" She shrugged in disappointment, and then pulled away.

"I am not sure what I was hoping to find. But I don't think it was a treasure map. I doubt pirates lived here," I joked.

"Ya never know…" Cat teased, her attention now fixated on the ceiling.

"I wonder how long it has been since someone lived here?" Erin asked.

"It was probably so awesome once," Andrea mused.

The exit leading out of the dining room, had an arched beam of wood carved to look like a scroll, above which was mounted a vivid panel of stained glass featuring green leaves and red flower petals bordered by long rectangles of various blues.

"Oooh, that is beautiful," I sighed, awestruck. Sounds of adoration from the other girls affirmed that they thought so as well.

We were just about to pass beneath when we halted simultaneously, like we'd run into an invisible force field: spider webs swept across the archway. Chris was pushed forward ahead of us, our sacrificial pawn to remove the offenders and their webs of terror before we would agree to leave the room.

"This is going to be a long day," Chris sighed.

"Damn, dudes!" Kevin said loudly over the music in his headphones while looking down at his watch. "It's already noon. Let's find a place to sit down and eat lunch."

"Finally!" Cat said with excitement.

The archway led into the foyer, where the pattern of hardwood flooring had changed from squares to long planks running vertically inward. The shape of a large rug, long gone, discolored a section in front of the main door. The door had a header arch that was boarded over from the outside. On either side of the front door were panels where glass once was but now were also boarded over. From the front door, following the line of vertical wood planks, a discolored strip led towards the stairs which went up to the next level.

Along the lower portion of the walls ran wood wainscoting. It consisted of repeating vertical panels inset with relief sculptures of vases with flowers flowing out. Above the ornate top cap of the panels, the walls were a dulled yellow color that had once been a type of wallpaper.

Opposite the dining room, was another stained glass archway opening into a parlor area. The ceiling was decorated with detailed plaster moldings of flowers. The flooring was the checkerboard tiling repeated from the dining room, reinforcing the sense of entering a new space.

There we faced a giant stone hearth that stared back at us like an open tunnel into an abyss. All the brickwork within the fireplace was stained in layers of black soot from all the smoke of fires past. The darkness appeared like it was trying to reach out around the corners like charcoal fingers. The ceramic tile border, painted in teal moons and gold suns, stopped the charcoal darkness from escaping.

Above the border was a beautiful mantel of wood with carved spirals that matched the scrollwork on the archways. Looming above that was a huge mirror, framed in the same thick carved wood.

"You guys want to stop here for a second to eat?" I asked, looking around for somewhere to sit. To the right of the fireplace was a curved bay with three arches. Each contained a tall rectangular window, boarded over from outside. Above all three an additional arched header of glass, these hadn't been covered, and beams of light streamed through them onto the dusty floor.

"Yes!" Cat responded without any hesitation. "I am DYING!" She gestured towards Kevin to hurry over with his pack.

Kevin and Chris each sat down in the center of the room, dust bunnies running away as they plopped down their packs. Kevin started pulling stuff out like it was a magic hat. First came Cat's lunch sack, then he pulled out a tightly rolled up blanket, which he flattened out on the ground next to him. He patted it to tell us to come over and sit down. The four of us each took a corner, taking extra care not to get any part of ourselves on the dirty floor. He took out his giant Swiss Army knife, two flashlights, a first-aid kit, and his lunch bag. A few of his cassettes tumbled out as well.

"Ooooh, let's see what you got there." I reached out and grabbed the tapes, "Blondie: *Autoamerican*. I don't have this one. I have *Parallel Lines*."

"This one has "The Tide is High" on it," Kevin stated, finally pulling his headphones down to be part of the group.

"Cool. Hmmm… oh, and DEVO. Love them!" I said. Then I asked as I read the title of the single track on the next cassette," And who is this: Madness, "Welcome to the House of Fun"?

"Don't you watch MTV?" Kevin asked completely shocked.

"I only get four channels," I said defensively. Kevin's complete lack of awareness that other people did not live as comfortably as he did - with cable television; VCRs; Microwave ovens; and Atari game consoles - could be a bit irritating.

Andrea chimed in, "Me too! I've only seen MTV one time at my cousin's house." She scooted over to look at what else he had.

"When I've gone to my grandma's in L.A. I can get KROQ on the radio. They have the coolest songs," Erin lamented, "I wish our stations here weren't so bogus."

"Split Enz?" I asked Kevin, inspecting the unfamiliar cassette. "How do you even pronounce this? *Waiata*? Wa-i-a-ta? Waia-ta? What do these guys sound like?"

"They're on MTV all the time," Kevin said. "They have crazy videos with super catchy songs and circus make-up. I think they're from Australia or something. My favorite song is "One Step Ahead"."

I picked up another cassette and read, "Adam and the Ants: *Prince Charming*." I started to chuckle, "Wow! Look at that outfit!"

"I love that one!" Cat exclaimed. "I've been listening to it all summer. You'd really like the music, Gwen. He is also really sexy in his videos."

"Sexy like Harrison Ford?" Erin asked. "How can anyone be sexier than Indiana Jones, or Han Solo?"

"Better than Mel Gibson as Mad Max?" I asked, pretending to drool. "He is such a babe!"

"I am going to marry him," Andrea declared.

"No you are not. He's mine!" I declared. We stared at each other like we were going to fight then busted out laughing. "And we are going to live in a mansion on an island in the Caribbean. So there."

"Big wow! We are going to live on an estate in France, and I am going to drive a red Ferrari like in *Magnum PI*," she countered. "Ahhhh, man, that game was fun when we were kids."

"Are you talking about the fortune teller game?" Chris asked, obviously lost in our exchange.

"M.A.S.H! Duh," Andrea teased. Chris looked at her, clearly offended.

"Mansion, Apartment, Shack or House… you've played it before," I reminded him.

Kevin completely ignored the entire exchange while he removed the wrapping from his deli sandwich, which had layers of salami and mustard. He also had a bag of Lays potato chips which were smashed and greasy. He opened the chip bag, and poured a mouthful of salty morsels into his mouth. He then took out one of his thermoses from the side pocket, and chugged it, leaving a red stain around his lips.

"Hey, you got something there," Chris laughed, pointing to above his lips.

"Ha. Hawaiian Punch!" Kevin wiped his lip with the back of his hand.

"Must be nice," Chris muttered gesturing to the lunch spread, as he brought out his bag of cold hotdogs, took one out and had a bite.

"My weekend job has been at my Uncle's deli. I get some benefits," he sputtered in between large gulps.

Chris pulled out a paper sack and handed it over to me. I divided everything evenly between Andrea, Erin and myself. Looking over at Cat, she was already half way through her peanut butter and jelly sandwich. "Cat!" I scolded like a mother to her child. "Remember to breathe."

"How is she so skinny?" Andrea asked. She watched in amazement, as Cat, done with her sandwich, began to unwrap the tinfoil from a covered treat.

"Cat," Erin pleaded looking at the shiny coating of the Ding Dong with wide eyes. "Please tell me you brought one for everyone."

I looked over to see what they were fussing over. "Oh, Cat. How could you?"

Cat giggled, as she chomped around all the edges of the Ding Dong, eating off the coating and exposing the cake inside. "Nope, I didn't bring any more."

Erin pouted, looking down at her sad little box of raisins, a few carrots and a dry cheese sandwich. "That is just cruel!"

Chris brought out three silver foil bags of Pop-Tarts, and tossed two bags at us. "Here, there is enough for each of you!" He then opened another Pepsi, took a swig, and handed that over to us as well.

"Wow. Thanks Chris! You're a life saver!" Erin said as she grabbed the soda first, and took a long gulp.

Andrea opened up the silver bag, and started to nibble at the edges of the frosted strawberry tart. "Oh my god, this is soooo good!" She closed her eyes and savored the sugar. "Why does this taste so good?"

I looked over at Chris and smiled, then patted the edge of the blanket next to me. This made him blush. Everyone noticed.

"Go make out in the closet for Christ's sake. Get it over with!" Kevin blurted out. Chris turned to him and socked him in the upper arm.

"Kevin, shut up!" I groaned in annoyance.

"Not cool, dude. Not cool," Chris said. He still took my offer, and got up to come sit by me, glaring at Kevin the whole time. I noticed Erin giving me a death glare, so I raised my eyebrows questioningly. She turned away.

Chris turned his head dramatically towards Cat, "So, how long you and Kevin been going out?"

I elbowed Chris in the ribs, and whispered, "Be nice. Don't embarrass her." Cat looked horrified over at Kevin, hoping for some sort of answer to deflect the situation.

Kevin looked at his watch, and matter-of-factly stated, "Since 11:05 a.m. this morning." He looked at her and winked, "There, I made it official." Cat's expression was no longer of horror, but of relief, and she was positively glowing.

"Cat, how long has this been going on, and why didn't I know?" I asked, while doing the calculation in my head as to what happened at 11:05 a.m. *Ahhhh, the train went by.* I thought.

"Ummm… Since the dance. We've been talking every night. We hung out a couple times." She chugged on her canteen of water, offering it to me; trying to play it cool, like it was no big deal.

"When you say 'hang out' does that mean, like, playing *Centipede* at the arcade?" Andrea smirked.

"I think it means riding the bouncy horse at the playground," Chris joked.

"I think it means eating spaghetti, like in *Lady and the Tramp*! Oooh la la." Andrea raised here eyebrows up and down with the insinuation.

"Hmmm…" Taking the canteen from Cat, I took a long drink, keeping my eyes on her the whole time. She wouldn't make eye contact. "11:05 a.m. is when the two of you were alone as the train passed by," I remarked, pausing for effect. "Exactly what happened to make it official?"

Kevin started singing, *"Wookin' Pa Nub…"* impersonating Eddie Murphy's Buckwheat character. He continued with, "She's Unce, Tice, Fee Tines a Mady…"

"OOO-tay!" Cat responded, holding up her hand with the "OK" symbol.

"God, you guys are ridiculous," Erin remarked in annoyance, still glaring over at Chris and I.

The rest of us looked on in confusion at the exchange. Clearly they watched that *Saturday Night Live* skit, but whatever secret code it was between them, was unclear. What was clear was that they managed to divert all our attention away from the possibility that they'd been making out.

Chapter Eight
Strange Occurrences

After we were done eating, Kevin crammed the dirty blanket back into his pack, followed by the Swiss Army knife, first-aid kit, assorted tapes, and flash lights. He pulled his headphones back on, and clicked play on his Walkman.

We shoved all our garbage into one of the paper sacks, which Chris crammed back it into his pack. "Okay, let's go," he said.

Across the parlor, a heavy ornately carved door stood slightly ajar. A strip of darkness between its edge and the opening beckoned us into the next room. Chris pushed the large oak door sweeping a freshly cleaned arc through years of accumulated dust.

The exterior wall of this room had a set of large paired windows, similar in style to the rest of the house. They were boarded over from the outside, like the others we'd seen, but one of the upper panes was broken. The smell of mold was thick in the air, because rain had been penetrating the sanctum of this room for years. Below the window frames were untouched fragments of shattered glass scattered amongst a few pulpy corpses of old books. Mildew stained and tattered lace curtains fluttered ever so slightly with each passing breeze.

"It's weird that this room hasn't been cleaned up," Chris pondered aloud. "The rest of this place looks like someone has taken the time to keep it from getting trashed."

Looking around it was clear this had been the library. Beautiful built-in floor to ceiling shelving lined every exposed interior wall. Each were fitted with glass paneled arched doors that opened outward so that you could retrieve a book from a shelf. Below the tall glass doors were cupboards, each with wood doors inset with a sculpted rose relief. We counted nine of these double door sections just along one corner of the room.

"If I were a ghost I'd live in this room *forever* and just read books. It's gorgeous!" Cat spun around like a child in a candy factory.

"Hey! Do you guys hear that?" Kevin asked loudly. He took off his headphones, listened, and then put them back up to his ears. He turned the music off, and listened again to the headphones. "Holy shit!"

"What is it?"Chris asked. We were all staring at Kevin trying to figure out what his problem was.

"Here, listen to this." Kevin put his earphone up to Cat's ear, "Do you hear that?"

"What am I supposed to hear? You have to push start, the music isn't playing," Cat stated.

"You don't hear it?" Kevin asked with a bemused expression on his face. He took the headphones back and listened. Then he pressed play, listened for a second and then handed the headphones back to Cat, "Now listen."

"There is nothing but static now. Is something wrong with the tape? Try a different one," Cat offered.

"No, you don't understand. Even after the static started, when I turned off the tape, there were voices coming through my headphones." Kevin looked at Cat, imploring her with his eyes to believe him.

"Voices? You heard voices?" Erin asked with concern.

"Well what did the voices say?" Chris joked. Kevin broke his stare with Cat to glare at Chris for making fun of him.

"Seriously, Kev. What did they say?" I asked, breaking the tension. "We want to know."

Kevin clearly looked confused and rattled. "I couldn't make out any actual words. Damn, that was the freakiest thing." He shook his head, shivered slightly. He put his headphones and Walkman into his pack, like they were suddenly dangerous and had to be put away.

Chris got out his own headphones, pressed play, and waited. We all looked at him in anticipation. For a moment he looked confused.

Erin flipped out her hands in question, "What?"

Chris frowned and looked down at his player. He pressed the stop button, and then tried the play button one more time. He turned the unit over in his hands, removed the batteries, looked to see if they were in right, and then put them back in again. He tried the play button one last time. "They're dead," he declared dumb-founded. "How can they be dead?"

"You probably had it on too long," Andrea commented.

"I put in brand new batteries this morning. I can have it on all day and they don't die," Chris replied defensively.

Trying to keep the group distracted from the feeling that there was something unnatural about the space I said, "Why don't we look around. See if there are any important papers or books."

Ignoring my attempt to keep the group on track Erin asked, "Is it normal for batteries to die that quickly?"

"Not if they're new," Kevin answered, "Really weird."

"Totally weird," Chris responded.

I pulled open the nearest glass panel door, and stood on my tip toes to try to see up on the high shelving. "We need to find out who lived here, to see if they had a little boy who died. So look for documents... stuff like that."

"Do you think they would have important documents in a library?" Andrea asked. "Maybe we should be looking for an office?"

"It's been a long time since anyone has lived here, Gwen. I don't know if there is anything to find," Cat said, as she looked about.

"There could be family photos tucked away or something, you never know," I said. "Just look, okay?" I squatted down and began to open the bottom cupboard door.

A loud *thud* echoed suddenly throughout the downstairs, we all nearly jumped out of our skins, and swiveled around in fight or flight mode, looking for the source.

"What the HELL was that?" Chris yelped, looking at each of us as if we had an answer. We all just shrugged, breathing heavy from the fright.

Cat turned around toward the parlor, and started making her way back. "I think I heard my name…"

"Wait, Cat. What are you doing? You don't know what that sound was." I reached out to try to stop her, but she had already walked through the oak door. Against my better instincts, I followed.

I saw her standing in front of the fireplace, staring up at the mirror, with her head tilted to one side. "What is it?" I asked.

"Gwen, come here," she whispered. I slowly approached and noticed a brick had fallen loose from the hearth.

"Is that what made the sound?" I asked as I came up along side of her.

"Yes, the brick fell," Cat replied calmly. "It's okay; *he* was just trying to get my attention."

I followed her gaze up to the mirror, and immediately jumped back and screamed! In the mirror was a man. I swiveled around to look behind us… nothing. It wasn't a reflection. He was just *in* the mirror. He had a full head of medium length brown hair and a large mustache. He was dressed in a 1970s brown leisure suit. The wide collar of a polyester print shirt stuck out over the jacket lapel.

"You can see him?" Cat asked in astonishment. "I thought I was the only one who could see him!"

"Yes! Oh my god, Cat!" I kept looking behind me into the empty room, then back to the mirror at him standing there. "Is that... your dad?"

"Yeah. That was his favorite outfit!" She smiled affectionately, looking up at him as if she were lost in a daze.

"Wow. I can't believe I am actually seeing your dad..." I said quietly, letting the reality of this revelation settle into my consciousness.

When I saw the boy in the forest, he had seemed as real as the people sitting on the train around me. The realization, over a long period of time, that it might have been a ghost, was a slow process. Standing there in that moment, staring at the ghost of my best friend's deceased father... well it was mind bending. Each moment the significance of this settled over me, the more world altering it became.

"It's weird that I am seeing him *here*. I always thought he was attached to *our* house. How cool is that, though? He's like my guardian angel or something," she continued, smiling to herself. She then turned to look me and said, "He's telling me we need to be careful, because there are other people in the house."

"He's talking to you?" I asked in a shaky voice, feeling actual tremors pulsate through me as adrenaline raced throughout my bloodstream.

Chris walked into the room followed by the rest of the group, "We heard you scream! Is everything okay?" He stopped dead in his tracks as he caught a glimpse of the mirror. He stood there with his mouth agape, in complete shock.

As Andrea approached, she asked Cat in concern, "Did I hear you say there are other people in the house?" She followed Chris' gaze up towards the mirror. "CRAP!" she yelled jumping back.

"AAGGHH!" Erin shrieked, after also turning her gaze up to the mirror. She looked around frantically. "Where is he? Where is he?"

"Damn!" Kevin yelled in response to Erin's scream, as he made his way across the room from the library. "What is going on?"

Cat turned to the group, holding out her hands up, "Guys, calm down! It's okay! It is my dad. It's okay."

"Your dad?" Kevin asked, and then turned towards the mirror to see what all the fuss was about. His jaw dropped opened, as he stared dumbfounded, "That's your dad…Your *dead* father?"

"How is it *okay*?" Erin screamed.

"Oh my god… Your *dead* father?" Andrea repeated.

"Yes. My father is dead, but I've been able to hear and see him ever since," Cat answered. "I can't believe you guys can actually see him. This is so cool!"

"COOL?" Erin screamed again.

"You see," I jumped in, "I *told* you guys...ghosts *are* real! Now you *have* to believe me. The little boy in the forest, he's real too!" I stated, no longer afraid, but empowered.

"Cat, what did you say about there being other people in the house? Other ghosts?" Andrea whispered. She held on to Erin's arm, both of them turning around quickly as if someone were going to sneak up on them.

"Yes, other spirits," Cat confirmed.

Kevin was still shaking his head in amazement, "Cat, I will admit, I wasn't 100% convinced when you told me you could talk to him. But that is *actually* him," he said as he stood there transfixed, staring at the mirror.

"Daaaamn!" Chris finally managed to say, as he too stood there staring at mirror. "Is this really happening right now?"

"What else is he telling you?" I asked, hoping that maybe he would help us track down proof of the little boy's existence.

"Just that we need to be careful, but he's not saying why." Just then he slowly faded from view, as if someone had blown out a candle, leaving wisps of smoke dissipating in the air.

"Did we really just see an actual ghost?" Andrea asked, completely awestruck at what she had witnessed. Cat bowed her head affirmatively. "Woooooow. I mean...just, *wow!*"

"Are you all insane?" Erin screeched again, holding tight to Andrea's arm. "How are you all okay with this? How is that even possible?" She let go of Andrea's arm and began to distance herself away from the mirror, as she kept glancing quickly back over her shoulder. "This is just a joke, right?" she asked, as she looked accusingly at each of us.

"Erin, try to calm down," I said. "We all just saw the same thing. I am just as rattled as you are, and I was the one hoping to see a ghost today!"

Chris tried to approach her speaking calmly, "No one is playing a joke on you. It's okay. See we are all okay!"

"I want to leave. NOW!" Erin yelled at Chris, as he closed in on her and tried to coax her back towards the group.

"It is broad daylight, and you're with us. Nothing bad will happen," Andrea said in an attempt to comfort her, holding out her hand and Erin took it reluctantly. "Right, Cat? Nothing bad will happen."

"Can we please just go? Pleeeeeaaaaase!" Erin pleaded, clearly only moments away from losing it.

"Erin, we will be fine," Cat offered. The sideways glance she gave me, however, let me know she was worried about her father's warning, and really didn't know the answer to that question.

Kevin took control of the situation, and started to move us out of the parlor back into the foyer, "Erin, we *will* go, but first we need check out the rest of the house, okay?" he reasoned, "We came all this way."

"Wait, what about the Library?" I put my hand on his elbow to slow his momentum. "We didn't finish looking."

"We can come back," Chris offered, backing up Kevin's idea. "Right now we just need to finish exploring. It's already darker in here than we thought it would be, in full daylight. It's only going to get darker as the day goes on." With concern in his eyes, he motioned towards Erin, who was being talked down from the ledge of insanity by Andrea. "Besides, I don't know how long she'll last before completely freaking out. It's better to keep moving and keep her distracted."

Chapter Nine
Second Floor

With renewed purpose, but still buzzing from our encounter, we made our away across the foyer toward the staircase. Chris was the first to ascend the steps, while Kevin waited at the threshold for Cat to join us in the foyer. As I came up behind Chris, I noticed the detailing of the oak newel posts at the end of each of the large banisters. They were carved in the likeness of a parchment scroll being unrolled, the bottom roll facing inward, the top facing out. Each spindle of the banister was carved like traditional Greek column.

I assumed, at one time, all these parts had been polished to a smooth silky surface, but when I put my hand on the banister it felt grossly damp. Little slivers of wood came loose as I pulled my hand away. A strange, gloomy sadness washed over me, causing shivers as I brushed my hand off on my pants.

Half way up the first rise towards a quarter-space landing, Chris stopped suddenly, testing the next stair tread. Cautiously, he put his full weight down on it, only to have his foot fall through as the wood gave way. He seemed prepared for it, and was able to pull back quickly.

"You guys, be careful on these steps!" he called out. "They didn't seem so bad when I came down them before."

I took each step slowly, avoiding the area that had fallen in. As I passed by the opening, I noticed a room beneath the stairs. "Hey look!" I motioned to the hole. "We should check that out."

Andrea trailed behind me, glancing in. Erin was next, holding on to Andrea, and passed over the opening quickly as if something was going to try to grab her. Cat and Kevin followed, with Kevin stopping to reach into his backpack and pull out his flashlight. He kneeled down and shined the light into the darkness of the secret room. "Cool!"

"What do you see?" I called out to him from a few steps further up.

"I think it is just a closet... can't really tell. Did you see a door to it when we were in the Library?" Kevin asked.

"No," I answered.

"Me neither," Andrea confirmed.

"I sure hope we don't have to make a quick escape down these things." Cat mentioned as we continued up the stairs, "Someone is going to get hurt."

We made it to the interim landing where Chris stopped again, holding his hand out to keep us back. He pushed the floorboards with his toe, trying his weight on each one. Once satisfied, he walked out onto the small space without any problem. Relieved, we continued to follow him up the second flight of steps to the right. The wood wainscoting from the lower level was repeated up the wall, following the incline of the stairs, and then the handrail finished off with a round carved rosette, at the second floor threshold.

This landing, at the top of the staircase, opened onto a spacious hallway, with diffused light drifting down from a dirty round skylight cut out of the high peak of the ceiling. The dust particles we had disturbed floated about in the sunbeams, producing an ethereal atmosphere.

"I didn't even know that was there." I looked up in awe at the window, and said, "You can't see it from outside."

The wood parquet tiling in the hall was a checkerboard pattern like the dining room, with a border that looked like an infinity symbol in a continuous chain. Down the center, where a rug had been, the wood stain was less faded.

The walls encompassing the hall were covered in a similar wood wainscoting pattern to downstairs, with the wallpaper above just as faded and torn at the edges as the dining room. The design, however, differed. It had a repeating pattern of dingy yellow daisies at the end of a meandering teal green vine, ending sometimes with leaves, and other times with a trio of gold berries. Several wall sconces were actually in place this time, two on each of the three walls that we could see.

Andrea and I got close to look at the details. Each brass sconce had two light fixtures that looked like candle holders, diverging from the base, each curving away in opposite directions. The main sculpture of the sconce was a mirror surrounded with a cherub on either side. They held the edge of some sort of fabric which acted as the design element to surround the mirror. At the top there was a mantel where two more cherubs sat, back to back, holding the ends of the fabric wreath, like they alone were holding the weight of the mirror.

"That is soooo cool," she said.

"I hate those creepy winged babies," Erin complained.

"Did they even have electricity back then?" Kevin joked.

"Duh!" Andrea responded.

At one end of the wide hallway was an open window with a half broken pane. Glass lay on the floor in front of it. "That's where I came in," Chris pointed out.

On the opposite end, it opened up into a bay room similar to the one downstairs. "That must be part of the tower," I observed. We walked into the well lit space to look around, each of us taking turns to look out the windows.

"It looked like there was a third story as well. How do we get up there?" Cat asked, turning around in the room.

"Not from here, I guess," Kevin answered. "Let's leave our stuff, so we can explore the rest of this level easier."

Chris had lingered back at the landing, checking something out. "Over here," he called out, and motioned us over. He reached into his pack and took out a flashlight. I walked back to where he was standing, as I overheard Erin quietly begging Andrea to leave with her.

"Kev, catch!" he yelled then tossed his pack down the hall towards Kevin, who turned around just in time to have it hit him square in the chest.

"Oof!" Kevin exclaimed.

"Hey, at least you caught it!" Chris laughed.

"Erin if you don't want to come, you can just stay here," I heard Cat say. "The rest of us are going to see what Chris found."

Chris pointed his flashlight up a claustrophobic passageway just to the left of the landing in a recess within the wall. It was narrower than the main stairs, and the space between the treads was tighter, making it a steeper grade. It curved to the left as it rose up, crossing over the area where the main staircase was below, in the direction of the tower.

He led us carefully up the winding stairwell. The air grew warmer and more stagnant with each step, until it abruptly ended on a tiny dark landing before a closed door. In the flashlight beam we could see an off-white door knob. It was made of aged and cracking porcelain surrounded by a dulled brass plate with intricate floral designs around the edges.

"Look, a keyhole. Is it actually locked?" I asked.

He turned the knob, and it spun loose and fell into his hand, "Nope."

Replacing the knob back into its slot, he was able to engage it to open, and pushed the heavy door inward. It creaked loudly in protest. Light from the third story tower bay windows flooded into the dark stairwell as we walked into the room. Chris turned off the flashlight.

It was uncomfortably warm in the closed off space. The floor was caked in dust, and cobwebs hung from every section of the ceiling. Kevin and Cat followed in behind us, as we made our way across the room to look out the large windows. One looked out across the park, one looked out over the roof above the front entryway of the house, and the opposite window looked out over the summit and down the ravine.

"I always wondered what the view would look like from up here," I mused as I looked down.

"Is this the attic?" Andrea asked entering the room, pulling Erin in after her.

"Andrea, please. I don't want to go in any more rooms," Erin grumbled. She looked in to the space where we all stood, her eyes darting back and forth looking for any sign of unwanted company.

"No, but I think there must be an attic above the hallway. Look! You can see the roof of the main house extends further over from here," Kevin said, as he pointed out through the arched glass header of the tall bay window.

"So how do we get over there?" I asked. I looked at the interior wall that faced the windows, wondering if there was a hidden door. I started pushing against the peeling wall paper to see if any part of the wall would move. Nothing happened. I dusted off my hands feeling disappointed.

"At least it has awesome views!" Andrea remarked while looking down at the park.

"How can you be enjoying this?" Erin asked her, not hiding her disgust.

"Okay, where to next?" Cat asked.

Chris pointed back towards the stairs, so Erin turned around immediately, and headed back down the way she came. She made sure Chris was right behind her, watching her back. "It's fine," I kept hearing him say, reassuring her.

Once we all managed to gather again in the large second floor hallway, it seemed we only had two places left to explore. Chris chose the center door, opposite the stairwell. He put his hand on the porcelain knob, painted in red roses, and tried to turn it. It was locked. He pushed in on the door, but it wouldn't budge.

"How can it be locked?" Chris asked, somewhat annoyed.

"Well then, let's try that one," I said pointing to the far left, at the opposite end of the hallway from the bay.

Chapter Ten
Secrets

As the sun made its way across the sky, light from the circular skylight had changed its course along the hallway wall. Sun rays also made their way in from the broken window. I checked my watch; it was only 1:30 p.m. I wound it up again, until it wouldn't wind anymore, afraid of losing track of time later on.

Kevin took the initiative, walking towards the door to try the knob. With little effort he was able to force the door inward. A beam of light suddenly burst through the shadows as Kevin turned on the second flashlight. He stopped, aiming it to the left, then around the door to the right.

"What is it?" I asked, as we all walked up behind him.

"Do you smell that?" Kevin asked, pinching his nose. I walked closer, then immediately backed away. The smell of black mold was overwhelming, but there was another pungent layer that I didn't recognize; sickening sweet, yet a bit like rotten eggs.

"What the hell is that?" Chris asked, also backing away.

Kevin continued to inspect the dark space, with one hand busy pinching his nose, until he stopped his flashlight beam on a specific spot, "Ah, a dead raccoon, I think. It's bigger than a rat. It's pretty gross... hard to tell." He started to walk forward into the space when he suddenly jumped. He teetered a moment, then completely lost balance, falling back on his butt.

"Shiiiiit!" we heard him scream, followed by the sound of wood crashing onto the floor below.

"What just happened?" Cat asked loudly with concern, "Are you okay?" She ran over to him to help him up.

"Wow! That was close!" Kevin let out a huge sigh of relief. "It's a small hallway. The floor is totally rotted. It just caved in." He climbed to his feet and carefully shuffled right, to the edge. Shining the beam of light into the hole he said, "Down there. I can see the door to the kitchen where we entered."

Chris crept past Kevin, even closer to the edge, and turned on his flashlight. First he examined the hole, and then shined his light across the small hallway. "There's a closed door on the opposite wall," he said, turning the flashlight to the right, "and there's a little dark space against this wall that looks open."

Turning the flashlight to the left, he said, "There's another closed door down this way, I can see the knob." As he turned back to face us he said, "If we hug the wall, we can avoid the caved in section, to go check it out."

I looked over at Andrea and Erin. Erin was backing away shaking her head, "No way."

I saw Cat look over to Kevin, who seemed to be recovering from his close call just fine. "Are you sure you're okay, Kevin? You could have really hurt yourself," she asked.

Once those words came out of her mouth, I began to second guess the wisdom of exploring the space at all. "I don't know, Chris, maybe we shouldn't," I advised.

"Yeah, you guys. It's not safe," Andrea said. Erin continued to just shake her head no.

Chris turned away from us, faced the flashlight back into the hall aiming left then right. He pulled himself around the open door frame and climbed to the right into the dark hallway. I moved over to look in, holding my nose as I did. I could see him carefully keeping himself flat against the wall as he edged towards an open recess.

"What is it?" I asked.

I saw him peer in, his face illuminated by the flashlight beam. "Wow, it's a set of stairs going back down."

Suddenly his face disappeared, and all I could see was his shadow on the opposite wall - then nothing. The sound of his footsteps became increasingly distant, until there was nothing but silence. Everyone waited in quiet anticipation.

"HEY!" Chris called out and it echoed up through the stairs into the dark space.

"Hey!" I yelled back. "What did you find?"

"I'm in the Library! The stairs lead down to a freaking secret door behind a book case. I shit you not! Come down here!"

"What? That's cool!" I yelled back with excitement, "But why don't you just come back up here!"

"We were just down there," Andrea moaned. "What about the rooms up here?" I heard Cat and Kevin agreeing that they wanted to see what was locked behind the door up where we were.

"Forget about all the rooms," Erin whined, "let's just go back downstairs and leave the house altogether. I'm serious!"

"Gwen, you have to see this!" Chris called out again.

"Kevin, can you shine your flashlight over here so I can see how to get to the opening?" I asked, beckoning him over.

Once he had the flashlight in a good position, I pulled myself around the door, careful to not put any weight on the center floorboards that hadn't already fallen away. I reminded myself to breathe through my mouth, to avoid the horrible stench of death. Once around the door, I pulled myself to the wall, like I had seen Chris do, and scooted over to the recess.

It was a false panel in the wall that slid sideways. I could see a narrow set of stairs, no wider than a ladder, winding down. "Chris, are you still there?" I called out, feeling fear starting to take over.

"I'm right here - just follow my voice," he answered.

I began my descent, both hands out on the walls, taking each step slowly, barely able to see anything. I could feel the continuous spiral with every couple steps I took, and a weird wave of nausea took over. "Chris?" I whispered loudly.

"Still here," he answered. "Can you see the flashlight yet?"

I took another few steps, fighting the urge to puke or panic, when suddenly the beam of light illuminated the stairwell. I was able to go more quickly after that, wanting to exit the tight corkscrew as soon as possible. Chris came into view with his hand out. I hurried towards it, and flung myself out the open portal into his arms. "I *do not* want to go into any small spaces again, okay?"

"Okay," he laughed as he helped me stand upright.

I pulled back away from his chest to see his face right next to mine. His eyes were closed as he leaned forward towards my face. I realized what he was trying to do, but I didn't know how to respond. I turned my head away instead, to ask him what it was he wanted to show me, just as his mouth came towards me and he knocked his nose against my cheek.

"Oh my god, I am so sorry!" he said mortified, blushing bright red as he pulled away.

I laughed, rubbing my face, "It's okay." I was embarrassed, and confused. This was new terrain. I wasn't sure where this new affection was coming from. He'd never hinted at being attracted to me in that way before.

"What were you going to show me?" I asked, changing the subject from the failed kiss.

He recovered from his blunder by taking my hand, pulling me over to another bookcase, and then proceeded to swing it away from the wall.

"What?" I heard myself ask in astonishment, as a hidden room was revealed.

Chapter Eleven
Beneath the Stairs

We could see an area of light above us, peeking through the hole in the step of the stairs. The pieces of rotted tread board lay on the floor.

"How did you manage to find this?" I asked.

"I figured if there was one secret passageway there might be another," Chris stated, as if it were an obvious deduction. "So I just pushed on a few of the cases and got lucky."

It wasn't really a room, per say, more like a large closet. The ceiling was slanted from the shape of the stairs, making the space very tight. Chris panned the flashlight beam around illuminating the opening's nooks and crannies. In the furthest corner was an old steamer trunk, with one wood box on top.

"Ohhhhh, WOW!" I squeezed his hand tightly, trying to contain my excitement.

He reacted to the squeeze of my hand, by assuming it must have been a signal for something else. He suddenly used that hand to spin me around and pull me into his arms. There was a sudden rush that coursed through my body from head to toe, causing a slight light-headedness. This time as he leaned in, he course was true. His lips pressed against mine with purpose. At first I was shocked. I wondered to myself, *is this really happening?* The longer his lips pressed against mine however, the more I willingly accepted the advance.

It wasn't my first real kiss, Ryan and I had exchanged many in our short couple months of "puppy love", but it *was* electric. It might have been the adrenaline rush from all the scares of exploring the house, or just the excitement of 'making out' in a secret hidden room. Whatever the reason, I matched his kiss with the same intensity, and responded to his hands pulling at my body to be closer to his, until we were just one entwined being.

We startled at the sound of footsteps coming down the corkscrew stairwell, and the muffled conversations as they made their way towards the library. "Will you hurry up? It is so dark in here. I can't take it, hurry!" Erin was calling out.

Begrudgingly we pulled away from the embrace, almost in a daze. Every part of my skin was on fire, and every nerve was tingling with heightened sensitivity. Despite being horribly confused about what had just transpired, I was hungry for more. It was like being given a drug and needing more of a fix so the high wouldn't leave.

"Hey, lovebirds," Cat called out, teasingly. Then she poked her head into the secret room - our secret room. As the other's presence encroached further into the Library, it felt like an invasion of the inner sanctum in a sacred place; defiling it. Time had been holding still, floating separate and apart from us while we were in that embrace… now each moment of reality crashed back around us, loud and ugly. It was agony to separate and exit the room. Gratefully, he did not let go of my hand, also not wanting to sever the connection. It seemed, at that moment, that if we could just hold on to the physical connection, perhaps the moment wouldn't be lost forever.

Cat let us pass by her, grinning ear to ear. "Sorry for the interruption," she whispered. She then stepped in, excitedly calling out to Kevin, "Oh my god, you have GOT to come see this!"

"You were right, Cat. There was buried treasure," I joked, as we made way for the others to have a look.

Andrea and Erin followed up behind Kevin, trying to peer around his large frame to get a peek. I could see Erin glaring at Chris as we passed by her. I heard her grumble, "You have got to be kidding me right now!"

What is that about? I wondered.

"Can you bring something out for us to see?" Andrea asked.

Chris was rubbing the back of my hand with his thumb, and it sent electric shocks throughout my body. I could tell he just wanted to be away from the others and continue where we left off. He spoke these thoughts to me with each stroke of his finger on my skin.

We made eye contact for a second, and I hoped he understood my questioning eyes, "*Is this what I think it is?*"

We watched as Kevin backed out of the hidden room dragging the large steamer trunk by its side leather handle. It looked really heavy, and cleared a path through the dusty floor as he dragged it out into the center of the library. We all gathered around it in awe.

It was easily 3 feet long and 2 feet tall, and looked to be made out of a dark wood; so dark it was almost black. The black was a bit shiny, so it might have had a coating of something to protect the wood. There were light brown oak strips around the edges of the lid, as well as running down the bottom half and around the bottom edge. In between the oak strips on the lid was a metal sheet of what looked like copper, with designs of lilies and roses pressed into it. Aged pieces of hardware were across each strip of oak holding it in place above the copper into the wood of the lid. This same method was used on the bottom half. There were three metal fasteners on the front of the lid, with the one in the center having a keyhole. Kevin tried to pry it open, but it wouldn't budge.

Cat had followed Kevin out of the secret room with the smaller wood box in her hands. It was a perfect square; 12 inches in each direction, and about 3 inches deep. On the lid there were three sections, each with its own wood design. One section was separated into two equal sized squares, each edged in dark wood, like small picture frames. One section contained a wood tile design that looked like flowers; the other had a herringbone design. The designs were achieved by using a blonde wood against a brown wood for contrast. The other part of the lid was just one long section with a design that looked like brickwork. There were no hinges, and there was no obvious keyhole.

Each side of the box also had a different design. One side featured a checkerboard using the same blonde and brown contrasts; one side had a chevron design with the V-shape in dark wood against a blonde background; one side had beige diamonds with dark edges against a blonde background, and one side had blonde circles with beige dots in the center against a brown background. Cat turned it over and over looking for a way to open it. Each time she tilted the box the sound of things clinked around. We were all intrigued.

"Maybe it's like a Chinese puzzle box?" Cat wondered aloud. "You have to push sideways on parts, or push up and down, until you do things in the right order to get inside."

"Well, try it," Andrea encouraged.

We watched as she tried to manipulate different parts, taking advice from each of us on how to try it in different ways. One of the top panels slid open, making way for the other two to slide open as well. Each of the sections was its own compartment with the same thing: keys. Two smaller keys were in each of the small squares, and four larger keys were in the longer compartment.

"Shazaam!" Kevin yelled, as he reached across Cat, putting his hand into one compartment to grab the smaller keys.

"Hey!" Cat complained, swatting at him to get away, but Kevin already had the keys and was trying each one on the steamer trunk lock. By the luck of the draw, one of them worked.

"Look at this bounty!" Kevin called out, as he lifted up the heavy lid revealing a beautiful light pink satin lined interior. As the lid came to a rest back on its hinges, plumes of dust flew into the air like smoke. We gathered around the trunk to look inside, coughing, and swatting away the dirty air.

Inside the trunk was another wooden box standing upright. It was a miniature cabinet with a keyhole in between two small doors, as well as a keyhole on a bottom drawer. Kevin carefully lifted the cabinet out of the trunk and placed it off to the side. He checked the other key he had grabbed to see if it would open the cabinet, and it didn't work.

"Here..." Cat offered, as she stood up, and brought over the box with the remainder of the keys. "Try one of these."

Kevin tried each one of the remaining smaller keys, until he finally succeeded. He opened the cabinet doors to reveal shelves on the inside of the doors, each holding several clear bottles with cork tops. Inside, the cabinet also had a couple of small drawers, each with a small porcelain knob. Kevin pulled open one of the little drawers, and it was filled with dried crumpled leaves. He leaned over to smell the leaves. He pulled back, perplexed. "I have no idea what that is. Is it tea?"

"It's a medicine cabinet," Cat stated. "Those are probably a type of herb used to make medicine for something."

"When did you get so smart?" Erin asked in annoyance.

"I read a lot. And you know, pay attention in class," Cat quipped in return. Erin was starting to wear on her nerves.

Chris and I had let go of our hands, as I leaned over the edge of the trunk to see what else was in there. Erin and Andrea crowded over each end of the trunk to have a look as well. Chris decided to take the corks off of each little bottle, sniffing, and trying to read the faded handwritten labels. "This one smells like almonds."

Andrea pulled out what looked like a hat box.

"Oh my god. Don't touch that!" Erin protested in disgust.

Andrea sat back to open it. She placed the box lid aside, and we could see that inside was a long black funeral veil sewn to the interior of a black hat. The veil was made out of a heavy silk that felt stiff to the touch. Tucked under the hat was a pair of long black gloves, each with four black buttons running down from the wrist.

"That's not creepy at all," Kevin said sarcastically.

Lying next to where the hat box had been were several pairs of delicate knitted white socks that would fit an infant, a baby's white lace christening gown, and an old doll, the size of a toddler. It had a porcelain head painted to look like real skin, with rosy cheeks and incredibly real blue eyes. The doll was wearing a satin and lace blue dress, with a matching satin and lace blue hat atop a head of long blond hair.

Kevin leaned in to pick up the doll by its hand, and it moved its eyelids open and closed. "SHIT!" he yelled, causing us all to scream in response and quickly move away from the trunk, as he dropped it back in.

"Crap, Kevin. Don't do that. You almost gave me a heart attack!" I chided, and then nervously chuckled at him for being so freaked out. "It was only a doll!"

"It moved its eyes!" Kevin said defensively.

"Those damn things give me nightmares!" Cat groaned.

"Aw, poor thing," Andrea reached into the trunk and picked it up. She straightened out the dress, and used her fingers to brush out the dolls long blonde locks of hair. "Weird, the hair feels so real," she said holding the doll out towards Erin.

"Don't get that near me!" Erin demanded. "That thing is disgusting, Andrea. Gross... put it away!"

Reaching back into the trunk, Kevin pulled out a mirror and brush set that was made out of porcelain. Each piece was hand painted, with a raised gold swirling design around the edges and down the handles. In the center of each piece was a detailed cameo portrait painted of a Victorian era woman. Each portrait was surrounded in a white halo ending in light blue edges, like the women's faces were floating on clouds. "Cat can you hold these," Kevin asked. "Be careful, they look really valuable."

"Awesome!" Cat cautiously turned them from side to side looking at the details of the portraits.

I noticed, as Kevin continued to bring stuff out of the trunk that there several old perfume bottles. Each bottle was a beautiful piece of art in and of itself, with intricate glasswork. One was a brilliant emerald green with a glass stopper; one was a subtle translucent violet with a metal stopper, and one was clear glass in the shape of a heart with metal top that had a tube leading down to a fabric bulb.

I picked up the heart shaped one, and gave the fabric ball a squeeze to see if any perfume would come out. A faint hint of an aroma wafted out. "Mmmm, it smells exotic," I mused quietly to myself.

When I went to reach in for another one, I noticed another wood box. This one was about 9 inches deep, 12 inches wide and 16 inches long. It felt pretty heavy as I lifted it out of the trunk. I sat down with it on the floor, in the last remaining shaft of daylight.

In the center of the dark brown wood lid was an inlaid brass oval. Two halves of the lid met in the middle of the design, with angled hinges on the side of the box, so that it could flip open. Each corner of the rectangular lid had a brass mount with a *fleur-de-*

lis design. There was also a similar brass inlay horizontal along the bottom. I tried pulling on that design element first, and it moved.

"It's a drawer!" I exclaimed, as I pulled it further out from the box. Within the drawer there were a few compartments: one held a stack of plain thick cream colored sheets of stationary; one held a metal 'calligraphy' pen, and the last one had loose metal nibs, for the pen. I closed the drawer, without disturbing anything, and flipped open the lid.

The two side by side doors swung open to reveal four graduated storage slots. One was filled with envelopes thicker than the stationary paper. There was an open compartment towards the front with dividers: one section held an empty black ink well; one held what looked like a metal stamp, and the other one had different colored wax sticks.

"That's one of those old English writing desks!" Cat declared, coming over to get a better look.

"How lame," Erin grumbled, while she sat against the wall with her arms crossed staring at me like she wanted to kill me.

Ignoring her, I picked up the metal stamp to see that it was embossed with a beautifully crafted letter 'B'. Then turning my attention to the sticks, I asked Cat, "What are these wax things for?"

"You light the end like the wick of a candle, I think, and drip the wax to seal the envelope. Then you press the stamp into the wax," she answered.

"Oooh, fancy!" I cooed. "I love all this stuff."

"Oooh, *fancy*," Erin mocked.

"I know! Me too," Cat responded then looked over at Erin like she wanted to punch her.

Andrea continued smelling all the perfume bottles, oblivious to the drama Erin was starting to cause. Chris finally managed to pull his attention away from the medicine cabinet, and walked over to join the rest of us.

"Any WEED in those drawers, man?" Kevin teased, putting on an accent.

"No, man... and you KNOW I looked!" Chris said in response to Kevin's attempt at imitating Cheech & Chong.

Chapter Twelve
The Locked Room

I noticed that darkness was starting to envelope the library. When we started out that day, it felt like we had all the time in the world. At that moment, it felt like we were in a race against the waning daylight, and that we had seriously underestimated how dark it could get.

"I wonder what the rest of these are for," Cat mused, as Kevin put the remaining keys back in the box that Cat was holding; two small ones and four larger ones.

"That one room upstairs was locked. One of those larger keys is probably for that," Kevin observed.

"Did the room remain locked this whole time because no one knew these keys were hidden under the stairs?" Cat asked.

"I dunno, but let's go back up to check it out," I suggested, eager to continue on and find answers.

"Oh my god, who even cares why the room is locked," Erin complained.

Standing up I then made sure the secretary box was shut and the medicine cabinet closed. I couldn't stand the thought of anything happening to the contents - it had been like opening a portal into the past. I started to head towards the hidden stairwell in the library wall. "Chris, bring your flashlight over."

"Wait, what about the rest of all this stuff?" Andrea asked. "We can't just leave it out like this, it will get ruined."

Chris impatiently said, "Just leave it. We'll come back for it." He then turned on the flashlight and came over to join me at the stairs.

Andrea propped the doll up against the wall, and stood up wiping off her pants. Cat began putting the mirror/brush set and hatbox back in the trunk next to the perfume bottles.

"Who cares about all that old junk?" Erin said, also standing up to wipe the dust off her pants.

"We do. You could help you know..." Cat grumbled.

"I just want to get out of here. Do you guys *not* get that?" Erin asked loudly looking around at us.

"We get it Erin. Believe me you've made it *really* clear!" I blurted out, feeling my anger rise.

"Go then!" Cat spat out, finally unable to contain herself.

Nodding my head, I said, "I agree with Cat... just go if you don't want to be here with us."

"Oh, you'd like that wouldn't you?" she sneered.

"What does that even mean?" I asked. Andrea came up to Erin and put her hand on her shoulder in attempt to tamp down the situation.

Kevin grabbed Cat's hand to lead her away from Erin, "Andrea can you calm her down?"

"Erin, let's go back upstairs to the tower, and we'll just chill out for a while. Okay?" Andrea asked in a soothing voice.

Chris then turned and started to lead the way up the corkscrew stairs. Erin reluctantly followed behind him with Andrea close behind. Kevin went next with his flashlight on, followed by Cat, then me.

As I made my way into the hidden stairwell, I had the eerie sensation that someone was at my back. I turned to look over my shoulder back into the library, but it was empty. I felt the hairs stick up on my neck, so I quickened my pace up the steps. I closed my eyes hoping that might stop the sudden onslaught of vertigo the winding staircase was causing me. I just kept my hand along the wall and took one step in front of the other until I suddenly found myself at Cat's back.

"Whoa!" Cat yelped. "Don't push, they aren't out yet."

I opened my eyes to see Kevin's flashlight beam faintly up the stairwell, and could hear him complain about how small it was and how he could hardly move. Finally Cat moved up a few steps, only too soon. The hairs were sticking up on my neck again, and I was on the verge of a panic attack. I was afraid I would feel something touch my foot - it was still extended on the step below me.

Not being able to move up until Cat had made more progress, I felt stuck, so I closed my eyes again and tried to focus on my breathing. In that heightened sense I suddenly was aware of faint noises below me, coming from the library.

"What the hell?" I shouted.

Cat jumped in front of me, startled, "Damn, don't do that. You scared me."

"Can't you hear that?" I whispered loudly. "There are noises coming from down below us. It sounds like the medicine cabinet drawers are opening and closing."

"What do you mean?" Cat asked, quieter this time, almost in a whisper. She had stopped. I grabbed on to her hand for support, feeling wave after wave of vertigo wash over me, and I was afraid I was going to fall down the stairwell. "Whoa, are you okay?"

"You don't hear it?" I asked. "You don't feel sick?"

"No, I feel fine!" she paused for a moment, gathering herself, "You're starting to freak me out a little, and no, I don't hear anything." She pulled on my hand and helped lead me up and out of the stairwell. "Let's get moving."

As soon as I exited, I breathed in deeply, trying to clear my head and stop the nausea. "Do you think there is anything in the house that is dangerous to breathe?" I asked, trying to figure out why I felt so ill.

"Why?" Kevin asked. "What's wrong with you?"

"Just trying to not pass out or puke." I sat down, and closed my eyes, "Give me a minute." I could hear the rest of them make their way to the locked room. I heard a small *'klunk'* sound from down in the library, and quickly decided to get up and join the others.

"Try this one," I heard Cat saying as she passed Kevin another of the long keys. A loud metallic click echoed in the hallway as the key rotated in the lock. Kevin turned the porcelain knob and pushed the wooden door inward. Light greeted us from inside the room from the large window on the exterior wall.

"Okay. That is totally trippy," Kevin remarked as he hesitated in the door frame. "Why has this room not been touched? Look at all this stuff."

SLAM! The door shut in his face.

"What just happened?" Erin screamed.

"Calm down, Erin! It was probably the wind or something," Kevin offered, trying to sound convincing. He turned the handle to open the door again, and it turned as if unlocked, but he didn't seem to be able to push it open.

Cat pushed past against the door with him, until it finally gave in and they fell into the room.

"What was holding the door shut?" Cat asked Kevin as they recovered, "And don't tell me that was the wind."

Andrea and Erin were already making their way back down the hall to the welcoming light of the bay windows in the tower, obviously not wanting anything to do with whatever was in the room. Chris stood outside the door peering in, appearing as if he was not sure if he actually wanted to go in.

"What is it?" I asked Chris. He pulled me up next to him so I could also get a peek.

"It's a little kid's room, or a baby nursery, or something. You would think someone would have managed to get in here with or without a key," Chris whispered back.

"Yeah, I have been thinking about that as well," I whispered back.

"You coming, Gwen?" Cat asked.

I stepped past Chris and walked in to a completely undisturbed furnished room, covered in layers of dust. It was amazing to see everything in its place, just like going back into time.

There was an old wooden rocking horse; a small bed with white sheets facing the window; a dollhouse on the floor in a corner; a small table with three little chairs complete with an old china tea set with three place servings; two bassinettes along the wall covered in a white lace fabric like a tent over the top of each one, and a wooden highchair.

In front of a small fireplace, there was a cushioned wood rocking chair next to an end table that had a small pile of old picture books. The floor was covered by an area rug with faded gold colored fringes. The motif of the rug was of gold rectangles filled with white and blush tinted roses with faint pastel green leaves against a soft pink background. This pattern was repeated around the exterior edges of the rug. The interior was a soft meadow green surrounding another center section with the same floral design.

Hanging on the walls, against faded wallpaper, were family portraits in gold painted frames. The wallpaper was a muted soft peach color, almost beige, with repeating illustrations of children playing outdoors doing a variety of activities, and of mothers with their children on outings. The illustrations were in soft pastel colors which created a very soothing atmosphere.

Cat was standing in front of a portrait on the wall, when I walked up beside her. "That little girl looks exactly like the doll downstairs," Cat noted. "It's even the same outfit."

Kevin recoiled, "How freaky is that?"

"Andrea said the hair felt so real. Would they use real hair to make a doll?" I wondered.

"If your hair was really long it wouldn't be a big deal, right? It's just a haircut, so why not use it to make the doll's hair?" Cat suggested.

"You don't find it ALL freaky that they would use the little girl's actual hair, and dress it up to look exactly like the real girl?" Kevin asked, astonished that Cat could be so calm and logical. Cat just shrugged with indifference, but I could tell she was deep in thought about something.

I looked around the room at the other pictures. One had a man and woman, with a blonde baby in the woman's arms. Another portrait had a small baby with brown hair in a bassinette. It was hard to tell if the babies were boys or girls.

"I still want to know, why is this room undisturbed?" I asked aloud to no one in particular. "It has to be decades since anyone has lived here, and the rest of the house has been emptied out."

"I guess, because the keys were hidden," Cat offered as a possible answer.

"If someone wanted in this room, they could have broken in," Chris stated.

"Well maybe that explains the door slamming in my face. Someone doesn't want anyone to come in here," Kevin suggested.

"Dad did say there were others," Cat said.

At that moment, I caught the scent of something, "Do you smell that? It smells like the perfume from the trunk?"

WHAP

The sudden noise in the room startled everyone. "What the…" Kevin exclaimed.

One of the children's picture books was suddenly lying on the floor, in front of the fireplace. Particles of dust floated up in the air playing in the streams of light.

"Okay! See I told you so!" Kevin quickly walked over to Cat, grabbed some keys and headed out the door. "Later days dudes!"

"Where are you going?" Chris asked.

"I'm going to see what the rest of these keys open." He had no interest in sticking around to find out what knocked over the book.

I pushed Chris' back towards the door, "Let's follow Kevin."

"Did a ghost do that?" Chris asked. "Tell me that wasn't a ghost."

"Okay, it wasn't a ghost," Kevin answered unconvincingly.

Cat was staring down at the book, but she wasn't really looking at it, more like listening to something, or someone.

"Come on," I leaned back in the room, begging her to keep up with the group.

"Hey where did you go, Kevin?" I heard Chris call out from the hallway. We heard Kevin's muffled reply from a distance. Chris followed the sound, and I kept close behind. It led us to the back hallway, with the hole in the floor.

Chris stuck his head through the door frame into the darkness, "Kev?" Chris called out, and then pinched his nose again, suddenly hit by the smell.

"Over here in this back room. Hug the wall," Kevin directed.

Chris edged his way out the door frame, hugging the wall to the left as he made his way to the room at the end. The door was open now, and some light spilled out, helping guide us, but making it painfully obvious how precariously dangerous the floor was.

Chris turned toward me, "It's not that hard. Just do what I do."

I followed after Chris as he disappeared from view into the open doorway, hugging the wall as he had done. I moved slowly, afraid the floor would give way under my feet with each step. When I reached the room, I was grateful to be on solid flooring again and to be greeted with daylight from the room's large window.

"I am not looking forward to having to go back down that hallway to get out of here," I exclaimed. "That was scary."

"Aaahh, it wasn't that bad - don't be a baby," Kevin teased. "Look what I found." He pointed to another door, smaller than the main one, in a back corner. "And guess what I have?" He held up two more large unused keys.

"So, open it already, almighty Key Master!" Chris commanded.

Kevin got lucky on his first choice, and it unlocked. He pulled back on the knob, painted with small blue flowers, and the door swung towards him. The space behind the door frame held a tall ladder leading up to another story.

"I bet that goes up to the attic!" I whispered to Chris, grabbing on to his hand.

Cat came up behind me, seemingly out of thin air, "What're we whispering about?"

Chapter Thirteen
The Attic

We each took turns climbing up the ladder, until we pulled ourselves up into the attic space. The heat of the day was oppressive. The only light came from a small round window at the end of the long triangular room.

Kevin was able to stand up in the center, at the highest peak of the roofline. He walked toward the window to see if it would open. It swiveled on a middle section so that the top half swung in the room, and the bottom half swung out. He turned to face us and moved the beam of his flashlight around the room for us to take in the surroundings.

"Are Andrea and Erin behind you?" I asked Cat, looking down the ladder, waiting.

"No, they are still in the tower," Cat replied. "Guarding the backpacks I guess - which is probably all Erin is good for anyways."

"Aw, come on Cat, be nice," Chris said.

"I am a *very* nice person!" Cat responded, then looked back at me, "Hey, I meant to ask you if any of those portraits in the kid's room looked like your little ghost boy?"

"No… he was older," I responded. "What was up with that book, by the way? It just fell off the table! It had been laying flat."

Cat was just about to answer me, when Chris called out, "Look at that!" He pointed to the corners of the room on either side of the window where Kevin was standing. There were small empty metal cots stacked up on top of each other, three tall. "What the hell were those used for?"

"They are so small," Cat noted.

"It looks like this was used for another nursery or kids' bedroom," I offered.

"Dude, look!" Kevin exclaimed loudly, pointing his flashlight into the shadows along the wall. The beam lit up a couple of wood boxes stacked on top of each other, next to a pile of old books.

"Wait! Over here!" Cat called out, from the opposite wall, as she lifted up the heavy lid of a steamer trunk. "It wasn't locked. Look, it's filled with children's clothes, and tons of shoes."

She pulled out stained and tattered pieces of clothing: boys trousers with buttons up a side panel along the leg; knickerbockers that fastened below the knee; matching short waist jackets with cut away fronts and single fasteners at the neck; and loose billowy blouses with buttons up the fronts and the waist area, to attach to the trousers. There were also smaller sized white smocks and dresses with buttons up the front.

"Are those all boys clothes?" I asked, coming over to see the collection.

"Some are. I can't tell with these," Cat answered, holding up the small white dresses.

"Look at all the shoes!" Chris mused. There were slip-on baby shoes made out soft pliable leather, and some that had a harder leather sole with a flap that pulled over the top of the foot to button up along the side. The leather was dry and cracked. The larger boy shoes were laced up the front, and looked sturdier for walking. The soles and heels were almost worn completely out.

Next to the trunk was a wood rocking horse; a small table with a melted candle on it; and a crate filled with wood spinning tops, large marbles, a circle of paper with drawings on each side and strings attached on opposite sides.

Chris had pulled the toy out of the crate and was twisting the strings. The twisting of the strings made the paper spin which then made the drawings look like they were moving. "Cool," he said, as he held it up to show us how it worked.

"SHIT!" Kevin croaked, startling all of us. Then he chuckled nervously, as he passed his flashlight beam again back across a free-standing full-length mirror, and saw his own reflection.

Chris smirked, "That's what you almost did in your pants, huh?" Chris gave Kevin a knowing wink.

"Very funny...very funny," Kevin replied sarcastically, "like that wouldn't have scared you!"

"Chris, can you bring the light over to these boxes," I asked, suddenly distracted. "Cat, can you hand me one of those small keys? This one seems locked."

I had spotted a black mother-of-pearl inlay jewelry box. As I lifted it carefully from its spot, I noticed how light it felt in comparison to the other boxes we'd held. "What do you think this is made out of?" I tapped my fingernail against the hard shiny black surface.

"I dunno," Cat responded, running her hand over the beauty of the floral inlay design. "They sure did like flowers back then, have you noticed that? Everything has flowers on it."

Cat handed me the two remaining small keys, and I tried both. The second one popped the latch open after I turned it, and I was able to lift the lid. I was amazed to see a vivid purple velvet lining inside, with trays of velvet lined tiny compartments. Each of the compartments held a little trinket.

"Why would anyone keep these weird things in a locked jewelry box?" Chris wondered, as he held his flashlight beam steady.

I could see a variety of things: a couple buttons, a red hair ribbon, and some metal jacks. My eye, however, was immediately drawn to an oval shaped object. It looked like a brooch that had a sharp pin coming out one end. It was woven together with what looked like black and gold string. Each thread wove through a seed pearl, and in the center of the weaving was a mesh cage holding something.

"What IS that?" I wondered aloud, as I picked it up. A small strand of brown hair poked out from underneath the woven mesh of pearls. When I touched it I saw a flash of a child's face. I dropped the brooch back immediately, feeling uncomfortable.

Cat picked up a cat's eye marble from one of the tiny compartments, looking through it as she held it up to the flashlight. "Why keep one marble in a jewelry box?"

"Look, the top lifts off, and there is another tray," I said as I lifted off the top section. "There are tons more things in here."

"What's that?" Cat asked, pointing to one of several little cardboard boxes. I picked it up and lifted the lid off the box; it was filled with baby teeth.

"Oh, gross! Are those real teeth?" Chris asked. Cat picked up one of the teeth in the box, looking at it in the light.

"Yep! There is even old blood still on it," Cat noted. "What's in that little box there?" She pointed to another compartment.

I opened it up to display even more baby teeth. "Okay, that is too many. Isn't that too many?" I looked up at Chris and over at Cat for confirmation.

"Jesus, there must be a hundred teeth," Chris exclaimed in disbelief.

"We saw three children in the nursery room. But one of those babies could have been an earlier portrait of the little girl with the long blonde hair," Cat offered, "So maybe only two children?"

"How many teeth do kids lose? Does the math add up?" Chris asked, getting more and more disturbed by the find.

I was too distracted to do any math calculations, as I held myself firm against a sudden onslaught of images attacking my mind. Images of children's faces flashed on and off in my mind's eye, like a slide show. It was never the same child twice, and there were dozens of them.

"Gwen?" I heard Chris trying to get my attention, and I tried to open my eyes, but I couldn't focus on anything because so many different faces continued to swirl around in the front of my brain.

"I'm okay," I said after a few seconds of recovery. I put the boxes of teeth back in the tiny velvet compartments, and immediately felt a release from the fugue state.

"Where did you go?" he asked. "It was like you were asleep or something."

"Sorry, I just got lost in thought for a second," I responded. He looked at me questioningly.

"Dudes, you should look at the titles of these books," Kevin called out from the opposite side of the room. He was kneeling down with his flashlight aimed at the titles on the bindings. "This one is called *A Key to Physic, and the Occult Sciences* by Ebenezer Sibly." He chuckled then to himself, "Ebenezer."

Cat walked away from the jewelry box, to join Kevin at the books. He read the next title aloud. "*Borderland*. It says it's a collection of news stories about spirit séances, astrological predictions, psychical research findings, and book reviews on the occult."

"In a minute," I replied. I then lifted the velvet tray up to see if there was anything left in the jewelry box. At the very bottom were some linen handkerchiefs, with objects wrapped inside of them. I pulled one out and unfolded the linen. In it was a Cameo locket pendant, hanging on a silver cable chain. Using the linen, I carefully opened up the locket to reveal side by side pictures of a mother and daughter. They didn't look familiar.

"Oh! Okay... I am starting to get a theme now with these books. I think someone in this house was trying to talk to the dead," Cat said.

Kevin pulled out a piece of wood that had been leaning up against the wall behind the stack of books. "Cat, you are correctamundo!" he said as he lifted up a very old handmade Ouija board.

After folding the first linen back up over the locket, I opened up the second one and in it lay an engraved silver pocket watch on a silver chain. "Hey, listen to this," I called out. "It has an inscription on the back: *To Harold from your beloved wife Beatrice.*"

"I wonder who they were," Kevin asked.

I folded the linen back up over the watch, and went to pick up the third linen handkerchief. As I lifted it up, a pendant fell out that looked like it was made of a small perfume vial. Chris turned his flashlight towards the object at the sound of it hitting the floor, but stopped short. The liquid inside was thick and dark.

"Is that blood?" he asked. I am not sure he actually wanted an answer.

I picked it up with the handkerchief, being careful to not actually touch it. Holding it up against the light, it did look like a dark red. "Why would anyone have this?" I asked.

"Objects from dead people?" Cat wondered. "You know, like, items used in a séance to help make a connection." She looked at each of us, shrugging, "I am just guessing - it makes sense."

"And these teeth," I said. "They are from *dozens* of different kids. Why are there so many?" I was becoming genuinely concerned. "Were these taken from dead children?"

"It seems more like a trophy case!" Chris offered, as he shivered in disgust.

Quickly wrapping the pendants back up, I said, "This is really, really disturbing. None of this feels right."

I replaced the trays, and just before I was about to close the lid, my attention was drawn to the small cat's eye marble from the top. I wondered what significance the marble held, and felt drawn to it. I slowly allowed myself to make contact with it, and then held it up to the light in the room.

The boy's face came into full view within my mind's eye. The same round cheeks, the same big brown eyes, the same pouty lips – the boy from the forest. I closed my eyes and concentrated on him.

A vision of a big oak desk came into focus. A pair of little boy's hands came into view opening the drawers, searching for something. I must have been seeing through the child's eyes, as he pushed past documents, folders with papers, piles of white index cards, until he hesitated at the sight of a box. I could see the little hands as they lifted the lid of what appeared to be a cigar box - filled with train tickets. He then turned his attention back to the index cards and started looking through them. He turned them over one by one to see the pictures on the back side, finally stopping on one, and lingering over it. It had his photo on it…

I opened my eyes, allowing them to focus on the shadowed room. Everybody had stopped what they were doing and stood staring at me.

"Were you sleeping?" Kevin asked in confusion.

I put the marble in the front pocket of my jeans, and closed the lid to the jewelry box. I stood up slowly, a bit light- headed. "No, but I just had a revelation: we need to find an office desk."

"You did that thing again, are you okay?" Chris asked quietly.

"Yeah," I brushed off his concern, fixated on what the vision had shown me. "Where have we not looked yet?"

"Why do we need to find a desk?" Kevin asked.

"The answer to all of this might be in this desk," I responded. "Cat, is there a way to talk to your dad again, and get his help?" I asked.

"He's been talking to me this whole time," Cat answered. "There is *a lot* going on in this house."

Chapter Fourteen
First Contact

We stood in the center of the attic, where Kevin could stand up straight. Cat closed her eyes and held still. The rest of us looked at each other uncomfortably, not knowing what we were supposed to do. I was caught off guard when I noticed movement across the room.

"Did you see that?" I whispered.

"See what?" Kevin asked. Chris shook his head in confusion, and looked around to see what I was talking about.

I walked slowly toward the area of the room where the full-length mirror stood. I screamed, stumbling backwards, "Holy Shit!"

"God damn it, Gwen!" Chris and Kevin yelled in unison as they jumped at the sound of my scream. Kevin was holding his chest like an old man about to have a heart attack.

I was face to face with a woman staring back at me from within the mirror. It looked like she was standing right next to me. I looked around trying to figure out where the reflection would be coming from. I could move my hand through the area next to me where it looked like she was standing, but there was nothing there.

She was wearing a black long-sleeved mourning gown, with her dark brown hair wrapped high up on her head in a tight bun which enhanced the hardened stern look pulled across her sharp features. It was the same woman from the portrait in the children's bedroom.

Hiding behind the skirt of the gown was a young girl with long flowing gold curls, wearing a blue dress. She peered around the skirt, and stared back at me with large blue eyes. They weren't the eyes of an innocent, and the longer I maintained eye contact the more the girl's facial expression contorted into one of malicious intent.

I pointed at the mirror, hyperventilating. Chris and Kevin walked over, and stopped. They did not say a word, they just stood there staring, mouths agape, totally transfixed.

"Shiiiiiiiiiiiiiiiiiiiiiiit!" Chris finally was able to articulate. "Are we really seeing this?"

"My dad told me earlier," Cat interjected, "when we were in the children's bedroom..." she paused, eyes closed, "that she is awake now."

"What the hell does that mean?" Kevin asked nervously.

"We opened the box," Cat said, eyes still closed, concentrating.

"To be fair, we opened *all* the boxes," I responded.

"The mom is angry," Cat continued, in a daze.

"Can you be more specific?" Kevin asked, not averting his gaze from the mirror. "What did we touch?"

"These are ghosts, right?" Chris asked. "If they were asleep, doesn't that mean they would be at peace?"

"No. They are not at peace!" Cat blurted. "The mom is very angry that people keep coming into her house. She is trying to keep something hidden, so she has been trying to force people away." Cat was now shaking her head, as if she was having a hard time concentrating, "There is something horribly wrong with that little girl."

"Clearly!" I said. "Just look at her. She's a monster!" The girl in the mirror had me in her thrall. I was horrified, but couldn't look away.

"What should we do?" Kevin asked trying to remain calm. "We can put everything back, and we can just leave. How about that?"

Chris agreed, nodding his head, unable to pull his gaze from the mirror. "I don't like the way either of them are looking at us," he groaned, growing ever more alarmed. "Is this who your dad was warning us about?"

"My dad says she did bad things, so the mother had to make it stop," Cat answered.

"Make *what* stop?" Kevin asked.

"Cat? What about the desk?" I asked, suddenly remembering what we needed to find out.

"Forget about the freaking desk!" Chris blurted out. He looked at me in annoyance, then immediately softened his face, regretting his harsh retort.

"Oh, man... I'm sorry," he apologized, reaching out his hand. The outburst had actually helped break the connection with the mirror, and I was able to disengage from the girl's evil glare. I turned to Kevin, who was still mesmerized, and pulled him away.

"Okay, quick. I know what we need to do," Cat suddenly stated, snapping us all to attention.

"What do we need to do?" Kevin asked. "You still didn't answer my question... What did the mom stop?"

She picked up the box with the remaining unused keys, and turned to leave. It looked like she had a clear plan, as she headed down the ladder from the attic.

I followed behind, sighing in relief when we exited the stuffy room. Chris descended the ladder after me, followed quickly by Kevin, who shut the attic door behind him. He then locked it, and pocketed the key. It was the first time he had relocked anything that whole day.

"Kevin, I am not sure that will keep the ghosts away," I reasoned. "They are ghosts after all."

"It makes *me* feel better," he said in defiance, as he crossed the room swiftly on Cat's heels. "Don't forget to hug the wall," he reminded us as he disappeared into the dark hallway.

"Hey, I am sorry I yelled," Chris said quietly to me, hoping Kevin would not overhear his moment of vulnerability. "I was a little freaked out, ya know. I didn't mean it."

"It's okay. I get it," I muttered.

"What do you get?" he asked, shaking his head in confusion. I could tell he was getting annoyed again.

"Everyone, but Cat, is here today because it was just *something* to do," I answered. "You thought it might be exciting, and maybe you all thought if I did this I would finally get it out of my system. You wouldn't have to smile and nod anymore when I talked about seeing a ghost, because maybe you didn't ever really believe me."

"Wait, what? No," Chris tried to interject.

"Now, you're all faced with a whole new reality. The world you knew isn't the same. My crazy musings are really true. That's hard... that's what I get," I finished before turning the corner into the hallway. Leaving Chris dumbfounded.

I hugged the wall, taking each step carefully, trying to hold back angry tears. When I came back into the main hallway, Erin and Andrea had joined Cat and Kevin. They were catching them up on everything that had happened in the attic.

"Do you have anything left in either of those Thermoses, Kevin?" I asked. "I'm really thirsty."

Kevin shook each one to see if there was anything left and then tossed me one. I took a swig of the warm Hawaiian Punch and handed it back. Andrea reached out for some, and Kevin handed it over.

When Chris came in to join us, Kevin tossed him his backpack. He didn't make eye contact with me.

"Teeth? There were children's teeth?" Erin asked repeatedly, as if her brain just couldn't interpret the words correctly. "You know my mom kept my baby teeth, it's really not that weird." She pulled a bent clove cigarette from her front pocket, took out a lighter from the other front pocket and proceeded to light up. Her hands were shaking.

"Sure, but with that many teeth your mom would had to have had fifty kids," Kevin scoffed. Erin took a deep drag and blew a billowing cloud of clove flavored smoke back into Kevin's face in response.

"Classy," he sighed, as he turned his head away.

"There were all sorts of creepy things up there. Who knows what kind of stuff that lady was into?" Cat responded.

"Why do you think the girl is dangerous?" Andrea asked in concern.

"Because, if the mother is protecting this place from some secret being found out, something bad had to have happened here," Chris reasoned.

"We need to do this quickly, before they can do anything to any of us. I know where we'll find some papers that can answer all these questions," Cat implored me as we all gathered together.

"Wait what?" Erin asked in disbelief. "You said we were fine before." She took another drag on the cigarette, this time her shaking seemed more like she was getting angry.

"Again, WHY do you think the girl is dangerous?" Andrea asked, growing ever more concerned.

"The ghosts can DO something TO us?" Erin asked, equaling Andrea's tone of concern.

"Your dad told you where the desk was?" I asked Cat, hoping that would be where we could find some answers.

"Not exactly," Cat responded. "There isn't a desk anymore. The mom hid everything to keep the truth away from outsiders."

"WHY ARE YOU IGNORING ME?" Erin screamed as she stomped her foot, and glared at all of us.

"Because you don't really seem like you are capable of processing information at the moment, Erin," Cat quipped.

"Chill out, Erin," I said at the same time.

"Don't tell me to chill out. I have had enough." Erin stomped again, turning away.

"Well you guys aren't answering my question either. So maybe *you* need to chill out," Andrea replied coming to Erin's defense.

"Girls! *All* of you stop spazzing out!" Chris blurted. "We don't have all the answers, because we are still trying to figure this out."

"Okay, so where exactly haven't we looked yet?" I asked, trying to keep us on task.

"You are not going to like the answer, guys," Cat paused, "the root cellar."

"Uh, no! I am *totally* not going down there," Andrea proclaimed.

"Guys," I called out, looking down at my watch. "It's already 4:00 p.m.! How in the hell is it already 4:00 p.m.?"

"If we're going to do this we need to do it now and just get it over with," Chris declared, clearly at the end of his patience.

"Teeth?" Erin mumbled in between drags. "So, the girl is supposedly dangerous, and there are dozens of kids' teeth? Was she killing children? Is that what you are trying to tell me?" she continued. "You are full of it!"

Cat sighed and shook her head, "No, we aren't 'full of it'. Now are you and Andrea staying behind again, or are you going with us?" Cat asked.

"Well I am *not* going down there," Andrea stated again. "Erin," she implored, "let's walk across the road to the park. How does that sound?"

"FUCKING FANTASTIC!" Erin blurted out. "Let's get the hell out of here!"

Andrea looked at her in shock, surprised by the use of *the* word. "Erin!"

"What? It's not like you haven't heard of it before. Get over yourself." Erin's face hardened, as she glared at the rest of us, "I think you guys are just trying to scare me, and I'm *totally* over it!"

Chapter Fifteen
The Doll

We all carefully traversed the main stairwell back into the foyer, and Andrea and Erin turned to head through the dining room to leave.

"Chris, where the hell are you going?" Erin called out in disbelief. "You aren't going to come and help us get out?"

"Hold your horses!" Chris answered in annoyance, "We're going to put all the stuff back first... then we will come help you."

The rest of us detoured quickly through the parlor back to the library, while Andrea and Erin hung back impatiently.

"Please hurry up," Andrea implored.

Immediately I noticed the doll was not where we left her propped up against the wall. Then I noticed that the medicine cabinet was open, and there were a couple medicine bottles out on the floor with their corks off.

"What the hell?" Cat wondered aloud.

"Remember me telling you I heard something... this must have been it," I mentioned to her. "Chris put all bottles back, I saw him do it, and I totally made sure the cabinet was closed. This happened *after* we left."

"Where is that horrible doll?" Kevin demanded. "Did someone put it back in the trunk?" He lifted the lid and peered in... nothing. He then began quickly looking around the room, peeking through the glass doors of the bookcase. "Seriously, where in the hell did it go?"

"What was in these?" I asked, as I helped Chris pick up the empty bottles to put them back where they belonged.

"This one has a label, but it's hard to read." Chris sniffed the cork and responded, "It's the one that smells like almonds."

"Oh shit..." Cat said. "I've read that almond is the smell of a type of poison."

"I can make out 'y' and an 'n' and a 'de'," Chris read. "Oh... cyanide. That's the poison stuff right?" He corked the bottle quickly, and placed it back in its slot, then closed the cabinet doors. The key still hung in the lock, so he turned it to make it secure again. He then handed the key over to Cat.

"We should put *everything* back under the stairs, right?" I asked.

"Yes, that seems like a good idea. But first we need to find that doll," Cat insisted. "Let's get this done quickly."

"Why were the bottles out and opened?" Kevin inquired, a hint of suspicion rising in his voice.

"I heard noises coming from down here earlier, when we were upstairs," I admitted, hastily trying to get everything to fit back in the steamer trunk so we could shut the lid and lock it again. "Someone, besides us, opened that cabinet and messed with the cyanide."

"Is that why the girl is dangerous?" Chris wondered. "Did she poison people?"

THUD

A sound rang through the downstairs, making us all jump. Both Erin and Andrea screamed from the parlor.

"SHIT!" Kevin yelled. "I wish that would STOP happening!"

"YOU GUYS!" Andrea called out from the parlor, an obvious tremor in her voice. "It's the doll!"

"Why is that *horrible* doll in here?" Erin demanded.

"Was that the noise?" Chris called out, as he ran out of the library, with us trailing.

Arriving last, I saw everybody, except Erin, gathered around the doll tucked into the farthest corner of the room near the fireplace. Erin was fuming on the other side of the room as far from the doll as she could get.

"Do you think one of the spirits brought this in here?" I wondered.

"I think that the girl is playing with her doll now that she is awake. It makes sense," Chris commented.

"So what you are trying to tell me now, is that a dangerous spirit girl is moving her doll around the house?" Erin screeched at the edge of hysteria.

"Be careful. Don't touch it! We don't know where the poison went from that bottle," Cat warned.

"Poison... What poison?" Andrea asked in concern, turning her head towards Cat.

"*Now* you are saying there could be poison *on* the doll? Oh, that is rich!" Erin's barely controlled hysteria with each new discovery was quickly turning to hostility. She just could not process the day's events - refusing to believe them real. "You guys are really trying to sell it now."

"You don't think she could have put anything in our drinks?" I asked, nervously pacing at the opposite end of the room. The truth of the situation suddenly dawned on me: we could have been poisoned.

"We were with the packs the whole time," Andrea asserted. "Nothing moved on its own, no one brought anything out. There is just no way anyone could poison anything." She didn't sound too convinced of her own logic, looking to each of us for confirmation, "Right?"

"We need to pick up that doll and put it back in the trunk!" Cat directed.

"Well *I* am not doing it!" Kevin declared.

"I'll do it," I said in resignation. I took my white windbreaker off from around my waist, and tossed it over the doll, carefully wrapping it up to keep from directly touching it. Once I felt that my skin was safe I carried it back to the library.

Erin, eyes wide, moved even further away from me as possible, wanting nothing to do with the vile thing. Walking in the room alone, I felt vulnerable. The light had become dim, and I couldn't shake the feeling that there was a spirit lingering nearby. From the parlor I could hear both Erin and Andrea urging somebody to help lower them out the back window so they could get out of the place.

"In a second!" Chris responded, "For crying out loud, you're *fine!*"

I carefully placed the doll on top of everything else in the trunk, and freed my hands from my windbreaker so I could reach up to close the lid. My hand inadvertently brushed against one of the long locks of blonde curls, and I was immediately enveloped in darkness. I could smell a hint of the perfume, as I found myself swooning into the black void of unconsciousness…

I watched as a group of children, dressed in their best Victorian era dress clothes, filed in through the front door. They were accompanied by a man in a mismatched suit of light brown trousers, a black coat and a small black bow tie. His hair was very short and oiled flat, and he had a long drooping mustache. He shut the door behind him as he entered the foyer, with his hat in his hands. He and the mother exchanged a few words that I could not hear.

She was wearing a simple long green and beige striped dress with long sleeves and a high neckline. Brown velvet buttons went down the center of the bodice to her corseted waistline, then the rest of the gown puffed out and fell loosely down to the floor. I could not see her feet, so she appeared to float across the floor when she went to greet him.

I wasn't interested about the new batch of children. I was mesmerized by the light that streamed in through the tall vertical stained glass windows on either side of the door. The center design within each window was of a blue vase with orange handles filled with red and purple Irises surrounded by green and yellow leaves. Around the center was a border of colored patterns – circles, diamonds, and triangles - sectioned off with red glass dividers. When the sun's light hit the glass in just the right way, rainbows danced across the wood floors and up along the walls. The children were stepping on the rainbows and ruining their dance. I hated them already.

The man with the oily hair and the hat in his hands finally turned back to the door, opened it, and without glancing back at the confused children, departed. The mother closed the door behind him, turned to the children and welcomed them into her home. However, her mannerisms and tone of voice betrayed her real feelings.

There were two girls with long hair beneath large beige hats. They were dressed in long dark coats that exposed only their black stockings and high button up brown boots. There were also four boys dressed in a variety of waist coats and knee-high trousers with caps on their heads. They appeared shy, with their heads bowed, and fidgeted with a nervous energy. The mother told them to follow her, and she led them through the foyer up the staircase.

I turned around at the sound of a man's voice to face the archway into the parlor. It was filled with lavish furnishings, the floors covered with rugs, the walls adorned with paintings, and everything well lit. A roaring fire filled the hearth, and I could feel its inviting warmth.

The father sat in a chair in front of the fire. He had a full blonde beard and a long mustache, with short wavy hair, and piercing blue eyes. He was wearing a long sleeve white shirt, with a dark blue bow tie that matched his vest and trousers.

Looking towards me with his arms wide open, and a loving smile upon his face, he patted his knee. I noticed, next to him, lying on the rug in front of the fire, was a curly blonde hair, blue eyed doll just waiting to be played with. He said it was a gift from him to his favorite little girl.

I remember feeling a moment of joy and affection, and excitement to be able to play with the doll. As I walked into the parlor I caught my reflection in the mirror above the fireplace... the doll looked just like me.

I was the little girl from the portrait hanging in the nursery.

Suddenly the parlor began to blur and the details became distorted. I turned around trying to get my bearings, and walked back towards what I thought was the foyer. Instead I stepped through the archway outside into the fields somewhere near the house. I was watching young children, alongside some grown-ups, digging at the dirt with hoes and shovels. One grown-up was holding a hand plow being pulled by two horses. Some of the children were bent over planting seeds in the prepared soil. They all were covered in dirt, appeared exhausted, and looked too skinny to be healthy. I felt nothing for them except disgust. I turned to walk away through the *fields noticing the details melt away around me until I came upon a cemetery somewhere in the woods next to the house.*

I saw Mother there, wearing a long black dress, with a black hat and a long black veil that covered most of her body. She was crying as she stared down into an opening in the earth. I noticed a very tall man with a dirty white beard and a floppy straw hat standing next to it with a shovel in his hand. He had on a billowy off-white blouse tucked into tattered beige trousers, and wore tattered faded leather shoes on his giant feet. He dug his shovel into the mound of soil and then threw it down into the dark hole. I heard a sickening thud as it hit something solid. I held the doll in my arms tightly, and I realized it was Father's grave. I closed my eyes against the sight of the earth being piled on top of him.

When I opened them again I was in the upstairs sewing room with lit candles on every surface. Mother, still dressed in black, sat at a table in the center of the room, with a gathering of strange people. They had their eyes closed, and were holding hands. Mother had her hands on a board with letters on it and books of the occult lay open around the floor. Her eyes were shut, and she had her head cocked back as she called out Father's name; hoping to talk with him. I felt angry that she was ignoring me again. She now spent all her time in that room. She was always ignoring me.

I turned away to leave, fighting back the anger, and found that I was suddenly in the nursery. I walked over to a white bassinette where a baby lay crying. Babies looked so ugly when they cried. I hated to hear it cry. I resented the fact that no matter what I did, Mother was always trying to replace me. I covered it with the white blanket to stop the noise. It wouldn't stop. I pressed the blanket onto its mouth for a long time. Finally the crying stopped...

I turned my head away from the bassinette and suddenly at the foot of the attic. I climbed the steps, and entered the attic space to see children playing with toys. There were cots lined up against the wall, each with its own bedding. Some children were staring out the one round window, trying to get sun on their dirty faces. Some were in the corner crying for their family. Why was Mother always bringing strange children into my home? I did not want them there.

I noticed a few of the children were sitting on the cots looking at picture books. I realized they were my picture books, and the toys were my toys! Rage boiled up inside me as I swatted my things from their hands. They all stared, cringing in horror, as I struck one of them over and over again across the face with a toy. I stepped back and looked numbly at my hand to see blood dripping from the toy...

I felt a sense of vertigo as the room began to swirl around me. When the spinning stopped, I was back in the nursery, and I could see the back of Mother as she stood sobbing over the white bassinette.

"Gwen! Can you hear me?" A distant male voice called out a name I didn't recognize. Where was the voice coming from?

...She turned to look at me as I stood at the threshold of the room.

"Gwen wake up! Gwen!" I heard the voice again. It sounded vaguely familiar.

...I could see the hatred in her red swollen eyes filled with tears as she came at me with her hand raised!

"Gwen! Gwen, are you okay? Wake up," Chris was calling to me from what seemed like very far away.

The images in my mind spun around like a tornado, leaving me disorientated. I opened my eyes to see Chris' face hovering directly above mine. "Are you okay?" he asked again, his face contorted in a way I had not seen before.

"Yeah, I think so," I heard myself say, but it sounded like it was an echo bouncing off canyon walls. "Where am I?" I asked. It took a couple seconds until the sound in the room started to contract back into an enclosed space, and I felt like I was completely back inside my own body.

"Oh damn, Gwen. You scared me. What the hell just happened?" He pulled me into a hug, and I held him back.

I felt someone holding my hand, and looked to see Cat sitting beside me. "Are you okay? What happened?" she asked with concern.

"I don't really know." I stammered. "The last thing I remember was putting the doll away in the trunk, the next thing I know I am having all these weird dreams. Did I pass out?" I asked, sitting up on my own and looking around the room. Andrea wasn't sitting too far away, and she looked concerned as well.

"We really need to get out of here. What if something really serious had just happened to you?" she said, looking at me with a mixture of relief and fear.

Kevin was pushing the steamer trunk back under the stairs in the hidden room. He was just about to shut the bookcase door when he looked at Cat and asked, "Are you going to put the puzzle box under the stairs?"

"Not yet. We still have to a few places to check out - better to be safe than sorry," Cat stated.

He walked over to where we sat and looked at me, "You going to be okay, Gwen?" he asked softly.

"Yes, I am going to be okay." Chris helped me stand up, and made sure I was steady.

Kevin then handed Cat the steamer trunk key. "Do you have all of them now?"

"Crap," she answered, "we left a key in the nursery door. But that's okay. Do you have the attic key?" Kevin pulled it from his pocket and handed it to her. "And the jewelry box one is here... I think that's it."

Kevin then shut the hidden room, and we all walked back into the parlor, and met up with Erin and Andrea waiting for us in the foyer.

"It's about time," Erin complained.

We headed back through the dining room, and Kevin stopped at the entrance into the back hallway to turn on his flashlight. He went to lead us out of the dining room, but as we rounded the corner, we all came to a stop behind him. Illuminated within the beam of light was an unexpected sight. There was a hole in the ceiling, and piled up on the floor below, were broken bits of rotted wood.

He started to walk forward, heading towards the kitchen, but stopped suddenly. "Damn it," he muttered, shining his light at the debris.

"What's wrong?" Chris asked.

"I think the impact from the wood falling down broke these floor boards. Let me just make sure." He stepped forward more cautiously, pushing the ceiling debris aside with his foot. There was a cracked floorboard dead in the center. "Okay, walk along the edges, not down the center."

Andrea and Erin had gone in behind Kevin, wanting desperately to leave the house. They followed him carefully into the doorway of what used to be the kitchen. Cat and I followed the same path and Chris brought up the rear.

Once gathered in the kitchen, Kevin helped Andrea and Erin escape back through the window, easing them down to solid ground. The relief on their faces was evident.

"You're just going across the road to the park, right?" I asked as I leaned out the crumbling window, "And you'll stay there?"

"Yes," Andrea replied.

"We'll meet you over there in just a few minutes after we check out the cellar, okay? Stay where we can find you." I said, feeling a bit of apprehension

147

that we were separating - they were, in a way, my responsibility.

"Okay!" Andrea responded. Erin had already lit up another Clove and was storming off around the other side of the house to be as far away from it as she could get.

When I turned back into the kitchen to face the others, the reality of it hit me all over again. One part of me really wanted to crawl out the window after them and be done with it all, but another part of me needed to know what was going on. I knew I would never get that opportunity again.

"Why are we going to the cellar, exactly?" Kevin asked.

"It's where my dad told me we had to go if we wanted answers," Cat responded.

"Okay, to the cellar it is then," I said turning to make my way across the kitchen.

"Hold on, let me go first," Chris said.

The room would have been totally dark, had the flashlights not been on. The tall trees shading the back of the house made it seem like it was already night time.

"Careful," Chris said. I followed slowly behind him, as we crossed the kitchen cautious of each step on the spongy wood flooring.

Chapter Sixteen
The Cellar

Chris lingered in the hall, at the top of the cellar stairs, until I was next to him. He held out his hand for me to take. "You okay?" he asked. I could tell he was still worried about my episode from earlier. I took the moment to really look at him for the first time in hours, and it reminded me that he had meant the world to me for a lot longer than that short afternoon.

"Yeah, I'm okay," I smiled back at him. I gripped his hand tightly as we stood in the door frame, the door hanging loose on its rusted hinges, and stared down into the darkness of the root cellar.

The flashlight bobbed up and down with each step he took forward. I grasped tightly to the back of his shirt, as I took each step in turn. Once we both were standing firmly on solid ground, Chris moved the beam of light around to take in the surroundings.

The area was dank and muggy, smelling of mildew and decay. At one time there had been shelves, but most of them had fallen apart toppling over old food jars filled with dark gelatinous fluids.

Some jars had broken open a long time ago, exposing an indescribable dried-up substance.

"What's it like down there?" Cat called out as she poked her head in.

"Don't be such babies, and come down here yourselves to find out," Chris challenged.

"Why don't you shove it, Chris," Kevin responded, as he followed up the rear behind Cat, his flashlight bobbing up and down with each step.

There were stacks of cut wood for the fireplace, riddled with large spiders scurrying about. The spiders' old webs hung from the ceilings, in the corners, across the piles of wood, and all over the old shelving. It was a horror scene straight out of the movie 'Kingdom of the Spiders', which had terrified me - Tarantulas had taken over an entire town, covering everything in their webs, including the people.

"God, I hate spiders!" I shivered, trying to keep myself in the very center away from anything that might be able to crawl on me.

"Spiders... Why does it always have to be spiders?" Kevin mused, as he and Cat joined us.

"I think you mean snakes, Indiana," Chris teased.

He moved the flashlight around the room illuminating the darkest nooks. "Okay, I think I got something!" he proclaimed. We all looked over to where his beam of light was shining.

"That's it." Cat handed me the puzzle box to hold, as she walked over.

"What is it?" I asked.

She maneuvered the arm of her sweater to use as a glove, trying not to get bit by anything, and pulled at the corner of something brown. Chris came around Kevin, as he stood there with the light, and helped grab another edge to loosen it from its home. Together they were able to pry it loose from between the cut firewood and the cellar wall.

It looked like a piece of luggage or an oversized briefcase. Once we brushed all the dirt and cobwebs off, we could see it was made entirely of brown leather, covered with a waxy coating. The wax might have been used as a preservative or waterproofing at one time. It was wrapped with two buckled straps on either end, and under the handle was a small flap covered keyhole.

"Let's see if one of those small keys works for this," Cat said to me, motioning for me to hand her the box.

"Do you remember which one hasn't been used yet?" I asked.

"No, Crap!" she groaned. "I'll have to try each one. There are only four small enough," Cat noted, as she took out one key at a time and tried each of them. I could tell she was getting frustrated as each one she tried failed to disengage the locking mechanism.

"Here, let me try," Kevin urged, gently moving her aside and taking over.

"Hey, I was doing it," Cat growled, as she swatted at Kevin's arm. "You're not going to have any better luck," she challenged.

He didn't, and he offered the keys to Chris, who also had no luck. "Is there anything in here we could smash the lock with?" Chris asked.

"What about your Swiss Army knife, boy scout?" I teased at Kevin. "Is there a lock picking gadget?"

"I wonder why none of these keys worked?" Cat sat there in confusion staring into the puzzle box. "What was the last small one for then?"

"Well, this was hidden pretty well," Chris patted the case. "I don't think anyone wanted it found, let alone opened."

Kevin dropped his pack onto the dirty cellar floor, dug his hand into it and after a few moments of rummaging pulled out his Swiss Army knife. "Oh, hey!" he exclaimed as he flicked through each of the attachments.

"Don't tell me you actually have a lock pick?" I asked in amazement.

"No, but I have an actual knife. I can just cut through the leather. It's not like it matters anymore to anyone." Kevin held up a large blade. Then he shook his head, and flicked through the tools again until he settled on a different one with tons of sharp teeth down one side, "Ahhh, this one could work."

He squatted down over the case and started stabbing into the top until there was enough of a slit to use the serrated edge to start sawing away at the old leather.

"Hey, it's working!" I cried out. The excitement of discovery suddenly overcame me, as I began to believe that the answers were almost within reach. "Ohhh, be careful not to cut through anything inside," I warned.

"Chill out," Kevin chided. "I got this," he continued to saw away at the leather, trying to make a long enough seam to fold it away so we could get inside. Within a few minutes he'd managed it. He pushed the case to the center of the room, and we gathered around. Kevin backed away, holding his flashlight up high. "I thought you might want to be the one to see what was inside."

"Cool. Thanks, Kev," I replied, trying to sound casual and not give away how excited I actually was.

The first thing I saw was a piece of parchment with fancy lettering. I read out loud what I could decipher: "It is a certificate for 160 acres of land from the Federal Government. 'Donation Land Claim Act'. It says 'In the year of our Lord, one thousand eight hundred and fifty one.' Oh, 1851. Okay... and something to do with it being Indian land. Um, I don't understand what any of this means." I put that page aside, and looked at the next document.

"This one is talking about buying 172 acres ... the year of our Lord, one thousand eight hundred and sixty eight... then something about $3,800 dollars." I put that page aside and continued on with the next. "This year reads one thousand eight hundred and eighty nine... oh, there was a fire. A new house was built over whatever had been here before. There are the names of the buyers: Samuel and Tabitha Jane Briggs."

"I guess we know who the house belonged to," Cat determined.

"So who were Harold and Beatrice then from that pocket watch?" Kevin asked.

"Good question," I responded, "and who were the mom and daughter inside the locket? They weren't the people we saw in the mirror."

Cat looked at me in surprise. "Oh, you didn't show me that," she complained.

"Sorry, you were busy with the books," I offered as an apology.

"What is that under the stack of papers?" Chris asked.

I pulled up the remaining pages to reveal another wood box, just like the one the little boy had shown me. I pulled it free from within the leather case, and held it up to the light. It had fancy script branded into one side: *The Havana Sweeper*. Below that script were three more words: *Cuban Hand Made*.

"That's a cigar box!" Kevin exclaimed. "I've seen one like that in my dad's office." He sniffed at it, "Still kind of smells like it too."

I noticed a loose piece of paper waft slowly to the floor, and land softly on the dirt floor.

"There is a little brass latch, with a keyhole," Cat noted, and began fumbling around back through the box, to find the remaining unused key. "Let's try this," she said under her breath as she put the key into the slot and turned it slowly. The latch released, and the lid lifted slightly. "Eureka!"

"What's inside?" Chris asked impatiently.

"Train ticket stubs," Cat responded, clearly underwhelmed. She continued to rummage around, "And..."

Kevin interrupted her, "Hey! Read this!" He pointed his flashlight on the floor where a flyer lay face up.

"It fell loose when I had pulled out the cigar box," I said.

"What does that mean?" Chris asked, looking down over our shoulders, as we crouched around the flyer, "Asylums? Outcasts? Like as in crazy people?"

W A N T E D

Homes for Children

A company of homeless children from the East will arrive

Friday, Apr. 28th, 1893

These children are of various ages of both sexes, having been thrown friendless upon the world. They come under the auspices of the Children's Aid Society of New York. They are well disciplined having come from the various orphanages. The citizens of this community are asked to assist the agent in finding good homes for them. Persons taking these children must be recommended by the local committee. They must treat the children in every way as members of the family, sending them to school, church, Sabbath school, and properly clothe them until they are 12 years old.

Applications must be made to and endorsed by the local committee

An address will be made by the agent. Come and see the children and hear the address. Distribution will take place at the

Opera House Friday, Apr. 28, at 1:30 p.m.

"The best of all Asylums for the outcast child, is the farmer's home."

Charles Loring Brace
Children's Aid Society of New York

"It mentions orphans. So maybe the Briggs' family wanted to adopt?" Cat answered.

My blood began to boil as I read the tag line at the bottom of the flyer. "The best place was this farmer's home, huh? I don't think so!" I spat in disgust.

"Why do you say it like that?" Chris countered. "They adopted kids no one else wanted. Obviously this must have been better than where they came from."

"That's *not* what I saw," I said defensively, then immediately regretted that I let that slip out.

"What did do you mean by that exactly? What did you see?" Kevin questioned, with a look of confusion across his face.

Cat turned her head towards me. "Why didn't you say anything?" she asked in an offended tone.

"There's been a lot going on. I'm still trying to figure it out," I replied defensively.

"Well, tell us now and let us help you figure it out," she encouraged. Cat understood, more than anyone, how it felt when no one believed you.

"Yes, tell us," Kevin encouraged. Chris nodded in agreement, showing me he was also open to hearing whatever it was I had to say.

I was amazed at how much that day had changed the two of them. They started out that morning as just willing adventurers, but they ended up being true believers.

I guess seeing dead people appear in a mirror will do that. I thought to myself.

Chapter Seventeen
Connections

When I saw the boy in the forest, it was the first time I realized that the sensations I experienced did not belong to me. I know that doesn't make sense." I was unsure how I was going to articulate myself well enough for them to understand. "It was like having feelings that made no sense for me as a person, or for the situation: I was happy, it was my birthday, I had my family, and I was having fun riding on the zoo train. You know, not a care in the world," I paused, to see if they were following along. They nodded that they were, encouraging me to continue.

"And then suddenly I see this little boy. It felt like his big brown eyes were drilling holes right through to my brain. My mind became filled with images of his loving mother and his siblings, and my heart started to feel like it was breaking. I wanted to cry. I knew he'd lost them somehow, and just wanted to get back to them. I felt how helpless he felt, how afraid he was, and had an overwhelming sense of loneliness and grief. It made me so sad. He showed me a brief image of a giant dormitory with rows and rows of larger boys of all ages, and then he showed me a shop where all the older boys were making shoes. Then there is a memory of hiding his face away from a group of snarling mean boys coming at him with sticks... That image faded and the feeling that overwhelmed me was no longer sadness, but of being afraid... in pain." Again, I looked at my friends, for reassurance. It was the first time I really had unburdened myself of the story... the whole story.

"Before I lost sight of him that day," I continued, "he had pointed to a section of track we'd just passed on the train, insisting that I look there. He NEEDED me to look there. He was desperately pleading with me to understand. I became dizzy and nauseous, but once the train took me around the corner, and we lost eye contact, all the images and feelings went away. I know he was going to show me more, that he needed to show me more, but we ran out of time. Something happened to that little boy, and he needed my help. So, you guys see why I have been so obsessed by this? It's been haunting me."

"Shit, Gwen. That's intense," Kevin said quietly. He seemed shaken, and I got the impression that, between being adopted and the day's events, he was starting to feel a connection with the boy.

"You know I understand." Cat reached over and touched my hand. She could tell I was becoming emotional, channeling the boy's trauma. "So now tell us what you saw *today*."

I gathered my thoughts, "Well," I began, "I saw the little boy again." They all looked at each other in shock.

"Where?" Chris asked.

"Not in person," I quickly clarified, "just a memory. It happened when I touched the marble from the jewelry box. It was his marble. He'd lived here, up in that attic, with those other kids. One memory I saw was of a room in this house, with a big desk, and he was looking through the drawers. I got the sense that he wasn't supposed to be in there, and was afraid he would get caught. In one of the drawers was this cigar box filled with ticket stubs," I motioned to it, and rapt, they followed my gaze. "In that drawer was also a stack of index cards. He was looking at each one, flipping them over, until he found one with his photo on it. In the photo, he was dressed up and healthier looking than he was in the forest. He was standing next to other kids, also in their best little dresses, hats and coats; each with one of those index cards hanging by yarn around their necks. There was a picture on one side and writing on the other, but he didn't focus on what it said. I wish he had. I started to feel sick then. I've felt that way a couple times today, sort of dizzy and as if I ate something that was going to make me throw up." I stopped. I was distracted by the sound of Cat rummaging through the cigar box.

"This is what I wanted to show you. Here are the index cards! Is this what you saw?" Cat asked.

"Yes! Wow." I leaned towards the stack of cards she was holding, as Chris and Kevin adjusted their flashlights. "That is exactly what I saw!"

Thump

We all jumped at the sound from upstairs above the cellar, followed by what sounded like something being dragged across the wood.

"Oh shit! That's not good," Kevin moaned, looking up at the ceiling. "Please tell me the little girl didn't just get her doll out again."

"We locked the trunk, right?" Chris asked. "Let's just hurry this along in case they decide to come down here."

Cat started to flip through each card turning it over to look at the corresponding photo. Some were individual photos, some were group photos, but the sentiment was the same on each of their faces...sadness.

Even those who managed a smile had vacant, haunted looks in their eyes. A few couldn't even mask their fear and confusion, forever caught in time by the black and white photograph.

"That's it!" I blurted out in excitement. "That's the photo... oh my god," I said quietly in amazement. "I can't believe we found him. That's him."

Cat flipped the index card over so we could read it. It was an identification card.

"How did this little boy end up here? He's not even an orphan," Kevin asked, sadness creeping into his voice.

"He had two sisters with him, too. I don't get it," Chris pondered.

New York Catholic Protectory

Reception No. A - 1016   **Name** Joseph O'Donnell   **Date of commitment** June 6, 1895
Age 6   **Date of Birth** Mar 17, 1889   **Born in** New York   **Sex** Male   **Color** W
Physical condition Fair   **Mental condition** Good
Education of Child none   **Religious Instruction** none
Father Michael   **Born in** Ireland   **Living** No
Mother Margaret   **Born in** Irealnd   **Living** Yes
Religion, Father Catholic   **Mother** Catholic
Residence Time of Commitment 1295 Clover St. New York City
Committed for Destitution
Habits of Child Good   **Brought in by** Mother
Visiting Card given to Mother
Sent to the
State Board No. 16745
Baptized at St. Raphael's Church. Child brought in with his two sisters, Catherine age 10 and Mary age 8. Father recently died of pneumonia. Mother is a pauper.

"When I had those visions before, I had been wondering how he could have been left in that awful place," I said. "Now I know it was because they were poor. The mom obviously was struggling after the dad died. But if he had his two sisters to watch over him, why did his memories show a giant dormitory with the older boys?"

"Yeah! That's messed up!" Kevin agreed. "Poor little dude."

"Maybe two of these girls in the group photo are his sisters?" Cat wondered. She started turning over each index card again, searching the names. "Nope, none of these match his card information."

"He was sent to this farm alone, taken away from his mother and sisters," I told them. "That's what I felt from him. It explains everything he was trying to tell me."

"But how did he get mistaken as an orphan," Chris wondered, "and sent all the way across the country?"

"His poor mom," Cat sighed. "How did they explain it to her when she came to visit? You would think she would have done something to find him if she had known there had been some kind of mix up."

"Or maybe because they screwed up they didn't want to admit they made a mistake. They probably told her he died or something," Kevin commented.

"You would have thought she would have done something if she had known. Especially if she knew *where* they sent him," I concluded. "There were some awful things I was shown about this place."

"Oh, you saw more?" Cat asked.

Thump. Thump. Scraaaaatch... scraaaaatch.

We all jumped again at the sounds echoing throughout the cellar coming from directly above us.

"Crap!" Chris exclaimed.

"It seems like every time we get closer to the truth, the more noises we hear. Have you noticed that?" Kevin wondered. "The mom might not be too happy with us right now."

"Go ahead Gwen, continue," Cat insisted.

"Well, I accidentally touched the doll when I was putting it away, and it made my whole body sort of freak out. It was like being thrown into someone else's dream or a memory. I was seeing things through the eyes of the little girl that lived in this house. I saw a group of children brought in and presented to the mother. They lived up in the attic, and were made to work the farm. According to the flyer, farm life was supposed to be better than the orphanages they came from." The more details I recounted, the angrier I became.

"That was not even true! They were worked hard, like adults. They were skinny and dirty, and had ragged clothes that just hung off their bodies." I felt myself holding back tears. "They weren't happy. They weren't cared for," I paused, to catch my breath and collect my thoughts. "The little girl didn't like having these children in her home at all. She abused them when she saw them playing with her old discarded toys. I saw her hitting one of the kids."

"Oh, that's awful!" Cat lamented.

"But I don't think it was just that she was jealous of the orphans, she was jealous of her own siblings. There was something twisted inside this little girl; she wasn't right."

"Was there something wrong with her physically, like her health? Or was she just twisted in her mind?" Chris wondered.

"Well, there had to be something really wrong with her mind," I paused, unsure if I should share all the details of what I saw.

"What? Tell us," Cat insisted.

"Yeah, go on," Kevin encouraged.

"I saw as she entered the nursery when a baby was in the bassinette, the baby with the brown hair from the portrait on the wall. I think it was her brother," I paused, "She put the blanket over its head to stop it from crying... she held the blanket over his face... until he..."

"Damn!" Kevin declared.

"The next memory was her mother leaning over that same bassinette sobbing... She then turned to me...I mean the girl, with hatred in her eyes and... came to hit me," I paused, shaking, "I mean the little girl. I was seeing it like I was her, ya know?"

"That is just *horrible!*" Cat moaned. "I am so sorry you had to experience that."

"Oh, shit... Dude. Did she like kill the baby?" Chris recoiled as he made the connection.

"Yes, I think so," I confirmed. "She also had a memory of her father being buried. There is a cemetery out there somewhere where the family members are buried."

"Okay, so if the little girl was killing her siblings and abusive to the orphans, is that what the woman meant by being dangerous? What about the cyanide? How does that come into this story?" Cat mused aloud, lost in deep thought. "My dad said she had to stop her. The mom had to stop the girl from doing something. That probably meant stop her from killing more kids."

"If the mother was bringing orphans into her home, she had to be a nice woman right?" Kevin asked, clearly thinking about his own adoptive parents.

"I don't know. It doesn't seem to be that way," I replied sadly.

"Did the mom kill her own daughter?" Chris asked loudly. "Oh man, this is some serious messed up stuff."

"We should see if there are grave markers anywhere around the property!" Kevin said. "If those orphans died here, maybe we can find their graves?"

Cat shook her head, "If her and her husband were only bringing them home to use as farm labor, and the little girl turned out to be a serial killer," she postulated, "I doubt she'd bury the kids in the family cemetery."

"The cyanide was used to kill Joseph!" I blurted out, when the answer suddenly hit me. "That's why I kept feeling sick to my stomach and dizzy. I think the little girl poisoned him."

"It was probably used on more than just him then," Cat concluded. "And that explains why this leather case was buried back here never to be found again. The mom never wanted anyone to find out her daughter was capable of those horrible things."

"Ohhhhh, shit. Those teeth..." Kevin groaned. The realization dawned on him, that those horrible atrocities had been committed within the walls of the house above them.

"It *was* a trophy box," Chris moaned.

Chapter Eighteen
The Not So Great Escape

Should we take all this stuff with us?" Chris asked. "It's like evidence to murder, or something, right?"

"My dad warned me that we should get out of here before anything happens to us," Cat reminded him. "So perhaps we should just leave everything where we found it, and get going."

"How does that help Joseph, or all those kids?" Kevin asked. "We need to tell someone."

"Yes, we need to do something," I responded. "Chris can you bring me your pack, please." I gathered up the papers from inside the leather case, along with the index cards and put them in his backpack, "Okay, now we can go."

"What about the keys?" Cat shook the puzzle box to hear them rattle around.

"Did we use all them?" Kevin asked.

Cat thought for a moment, "I don't think so…there is one larger key left."

I thought of the mystery room I saw the mother holding a séance in, and reminded them, "There *was* one more room down that back hall that we didn't explore."

Thump. Thump. Scraaaaatch… scraaaaatch.

"Shit!" Chris muttered, as he ducked down lower to the ground. "What the *hell* is going on up there?"

"I am *not* going back up there to check out anymore rooms!" Cat whispered nervously, "Sorry, Gwen." She closed the lid to the puzzle box, and tucked it under her arm.

"Me either! I don't *need* to know what's in that room *that* bad," Kevin stated quietly. "Besides Andrea and Erin are waiting for us. Let's *go*."

"I know you're right," I said, "But..."

"We can always come back another time," Kevin offered.

I pointed to the box, "Are you sure we should keep those, Cat?" I asked. She hesitated, clearly struggling with the right decision, but then she nodded.

"I have a feeling they would be safer with us," she whispered with more certainty, looking up at the ceiling to whatever was going on above us.

Kevin turned and aimed his flashlight toward the cellar steps, and quietly crept towards them. I followed close and Cat and Chris filed in behind me. He put his weight on the first tread and it creaked loudly.

We all stopped, and listened intently, making sure we hadn't been detected.

"I know I might sound like a broken record," Chris asked in a hushed voice, "but do you guys have any idea what could be making those noises?"

"I really don't want to find out," Kevin mumbled, as he tried the next tread and breathed a sigh of relief when it didn't make any sound. He turned around and offered me his hand, "skip that first one and I will help you up."

Once I was on the second tread next to him, he moved up to the next, again breathing a sigh of relief.

"Okay, Cat, give me your hand," I whispered as I held it out. She grabbed it, and I helped her up. "Go on, follow Kevin."

She took Kevin's hand and stood next to him. I then turned around to offer my hand to Chris, to help him skip the bottom step. Once he was clear, we waited as Kevin continued up.

Thump. Thump. Scraaaaatch... scraaaaatch.

"Crap," I muttered, leaning into Chris and holding on to his shirt. We held as still as we could trying to not draw any attention to ourselves.

Finally we saw Kevin make it to the top and shine his flashlight beam around the hall. Cat was then standing up next to him, motioning us up, as they disappeared from view. When we cleared the creaky stairs, Chris shined his light down the hall towards the kitchen door, and walked cautiously against the wall away from the rotted center floor boards. Once he was in the kitchen door frame he motioned for me to follow the same path, and he held the light up for me to see where I was walking.

In the kitchen Kevin shone his light around. "Damn, it's dark outside. It can't be that late!" I saw him look down at his watch. "Chris?"

"Yeah?" Chris asked as we walked into the kitchen, continually glancing back over his shoulder back towards the dark hallway.

"Is your watch working?" Kevin asked. "What time is it?"

"Chris looked down at his Digital watch, and answered, "Hmmm? No… it's not. How could it *not* be working?"

"What about yours, Gwen?" Kevin asked pointing the flashlight beam towards my wrist.

I glanced at my grandmother's gold watch, and saw that it was ticking away steadily. "Yep still working. Ummm… it's almost 6:00 p.m.," I answered.

"That's weird," Chris mumbled turning again quickly as if he heard something coming up on us.

"What is it?" I asked, turning to look in that direction. "Did you hear something?"

"I just feel like we are being watched," he shivered.

Despite hearing all the noises, I had an overwhelming urge to go back upstairs. Something was nagging at me. "Hey guys, do you think we have time to go back up to find that room?"

"Are you crazy?" Kevin asked in exasperation, trying to keep his voice to a minimum.

"You aren't curious to find out what was making that sound?" I challenged. It felt like something was drawing me back in. We weren't done yet.

"Gwen, if the spirits can affect batteries, slam doors, open drawers, and move dolls, they also might be able to hurt us. We've pushed our luck as it is. We need to go," Cat reasoned.

"But, what if we don't get to come back? What if the answer to helping find Joseph peace, is in that room?" I asked, my voice getting louder. "We need to go look!"

Thump. Thump. Scraaaaatch... scraaaaatch.

"No! No we don't," Chris said, grabbing my hand and hustling me across the soggy kitchen floor as carefully as possible. When we arrived at the crumbling kitchen window, Kevin immediately positioned himself to help Cat up and out. She handed Chris the box of keys to hold, before climbing out the window while Kevin held onto her arms. He leaned out the window after her, and helped her down slowly until she touched the ground.

Then it was my turn. I climbed up onto the windowsill, and immediately felt the pressure of the marble dig into my thigh. I had forgotten I still had that in my pocket. I carefully turned my body around so that my legs were dangling over the back of the house, and the marble was no longer pushing into me uncomfortably.

I felt Cat touch my foot. "Stop kicking, I'll make sure you don't fall," she called up to me. I held on to

Kevin's hands as he slowly eased me down until I landed on my feet safely.

The shade from the trees covered the entire back side of the house in darkness, but I could see the summit was still in daylight. "Oh, thank god it's not actually night out," I said.

"It's going to be really dark climbing back down the hill. I didn't think about all these trees," Cat thought aloud. She then turned to call out to Chris, "You can hand me the box now!"

Chris leaned out and tossed the box to her. "Gwen, catch," he then called out as he threw his back pack at me.

"Catch!" I heard right before Kevin's backpack flew out the window. I had only enough time to drop Chris' pack before maneuvering to catch the next one.

"Good job! All that Nerf football finally came in handy," Chris smiled, and then the two of them made quick work of jumping down.

"I am really glad to be done with that place," Kevin exclaimed, as he wiped wood crumbles from his clothes. "But I will never admit I said that out loud," he laughed.

"Let's go find the girls," Chris suggested, as he pulled his pack over his shoulders and went around the house to head for the park.

We followed behind, but as we rounded the corner we were greeted with Andrea and Erin running full speed towards us from across the road. "Run!" Andrea was yelling.

"What do you mean run? Run where? Why?" Kevin was standing there with his arms out, looking at them like they were insane. Then we all saw it, a security cart coming up the road heading into the parking lot of the park. There were no longer any cars, and all the visitors gone.

Andrea and Erin practically tumbled through us. "Let's go... let's go... let's go."

"Oh shit!" Chris exclaimed in a hushed voice, "What did you guys do?"

"We didn't do anything," Andrea said. "We were just hanging out, and then the very last family to leave asked if we needed a ride, because the park was closing."

"Obviously we wouldn't leave without you guys," Erin chimed in, oblivious to the fact that they had already done that very thing earlier.

"After they left, we saw the security cart coming up the hill, so we ran over here," Andrea continued talking a million miles an hour, completely out of breath.

"Did they see you?" I asked as I motioned for them to come back behind the house to hide in the shadows.

"I don't know. Maybe that family probably said something," Erin theorized, also out of breath.

"Where is the guard now?" Cat whispered to Kevin who was stealthily peering around the corner.

"Maybe we should go down the hill from here, instead of going back the way we came?" Chris suggested. He walked into the shadows through the trees to the edge and looked down into the ravine.

"Never mind," he said. "I can see the tracks from here, but that is a really steep cliff. There is no way you can make it down there from here without getting hurt."

"Who are you referring to?" Andrea asked. "You mean us 'girls'?"

"Those of you who do not normally scale down steep cliffs daily," Chris replied condescendingly. "Better?"

"And, like, you do?" Erin quipped back.

"Okay, jeez. What I am trying to say is, let's find a different way down!" Chris threw his hands up in disgust, and walked along the edge to see what other options we had.

"Kevin, do you see anything?" I whispered, trying to ignore the spat and focus on what the real danger was at the moment: getting caught trespassing.

"Looks like just one guy," Kevin answered. He's walking around, probably just making sure no one is still here, and he's been looking across the tree lines surrounding the park; probably looking for those two," Kevin responded. "He hasn't looked our way... yet."

"Maybe we'll get lucky and he won't come over here," Cat whispered, now leaning up against Kevin's back, as he kept look out.

"Cat, you STILL have the puzzle box!" Erin declared, noticing for the first time. "That's stealing."

"Yes, I do, and no one will know its missing," Cat responded.

"*You* probably set off a silent alarm in there. He's not looking for us...he's looking for *you*," Erin accused.

"So what did you guys find down there? Any buried bodies?" Andrea asked, ignoring Erin's accusations.

"No buried bodies - lots of spiders though!" I answered. "We found an old leather case that had a bunch of papers hidden away. I'll show you when we get back to my house."

Andrea looked pleased, "So you actually found what you were looking for?"

"Yeah, I think so," I said, slowly acknowledging the sense of accomplishment wash over me.

"Crap, guys, he's coming this way," Kevin whispered in alarm.

"Oh no! Where did Chris go?" I asked, looking around.

We all turned towards the grove of trees behind the house assuming that is where Chris went, and so we all headed that way, deep into their midst. We stopped at the edge of the cliff and looked left and right, but couldn't see Chris anywhere. Where the stand of trees ended, the ground fell away steeply. While not a vertical drop it was still too steep to see down unless you got right to the edge.

Behind us we could hear the heavy thud of boots and the crunching of the dried grass as the security guard walked from the road towards the house.

"Shit! Shit! Shit!" Erin whispered frantically. "Where should we go?"

"We go over the edge and just flatten ourselves against the cliff face, just like when the train passed by. Hug the wall basically," Kevin suggested.

"How are we going to do that without falling all the way down?" Erin asked.

Before Kevin could answer, I saw Cat already down on all fours, swinging her legs over the ledge and digging into the dirt with her hands so she wouldn't slip. Kevin immediately trotted over, squatted and held on to her hands to ease her down.

"I guess that answers that question," Andrea said. She got down on all fours, just like Cat, and tried a section of the ledge herself. Erin followed Andrea to the same area, and they both tried to find some sort of footing on the other side.

The sound of thudding and crunching got louder as the security guard was coming around the house. I knew he would discover the open window leading into the kitchen eventually. The question in my mind was, would he look inside the house, or would he turn to the woods where we were hiding?

"Quick, he's coming. Go! Go!" I urged them over the side, and scrambled to where Kevin was climbing down after Cat. I couldn't see Chris anywhere. I didn't want to leave him behind, but he didn't seem too worried about ditching us. Every man for themselves, I guess.

That's when I noticed movement to my right along the steep face of the cliff. I thought it might be Chris, so I spider crawled along the edge, staying as low to the ground as possible.

I could hear the frantic whispers of my friends behind me as I crawled away from the house no longer in the safety of the shadows from the trees.

I stopped when I realized I either had to climb over the ledge right then and there and wait out the security guard, or I had to make a run for it to the spot where I saw the movement, and then climb over.

I was about to jump up, prepared to dash, when I heard Chris whisper my name. I was confused to realize he was right near me hanging on the edge of the steep bramble covered incline. I wondered then, if the movement over there hadn't been Chris...

"Down here," he said, as his hand reached out from the shadows towards mine.

I swung my legs over the ledge and tried to find footholds as I climbed down. I could feel Chris' hands on my legs, helping guide me down to where he was hiding. "I got ya," he whispered.

I had just got my head down below the lip, when I heard the security guard call out. I brought my hands down off the ledge and curled up into Chris arms.

The bushes, which had taken root deep in the dirt of the rocky face, were all that stood between us and a long tumble. He held us there as flat against the cliff side as we could get.

I could feel the heat from his breath against my cheek, and feel his chest rising and falling. For one second, with my eyes closed, everything else fell away, and it was just the two of us. I remembered the kiss, and wondered about the possibilities once we made it back home…

"Did he see you?" Chris whispered in my ear.

"I don't know. Can you tell if he is coming this way?" I whispered back. Pebbles tumbled free from the roots with each moment we stood there, barely holding our weight. My feet kept slipping out from under me, and I would have to reposition, making even more rocks fall away.

"It sounded like he was still back towards the house. Maybe he was calling out to one of the others. Hold on, let me check," he turned to face the cliff side, and hoisted himself up just enough to look up over the edge. "Oh crap!"

"What?" I whispered in alarm.

"Quick, duck down over there. Don't move and don't make a sound," he pointed to a dark shadow beneath a cluster of bushes and young saplings to our left. I did as he instructed and scaled my way along the cliff, slipping every couple of inches, until I made it into the shadows. He unshouldered his pack, and used his foot to push it towards me as quietly as possible. I grabbed it and pulled it in.

My adrenaline was pumping, and I was trying to slow my breathing down, afraid that the guard would hear me. I closed my arms around my legs, hugging his backpack to my stomach. I put my head on my knees and watched as my worse fear unfolded.

I saw him scoot along the cliff wall in the opposite direction, further and further away from the house. He found some solid ground, and was able to run a little further, before the security guard peered over the edge and caught sight of him.

"Hey, kid! You know I can see you, right?" the security guard called out. "Why don't you just make this easier on yourself, and climb on up here."

I saw Chris stop, and breathe out a deep sigh in resignation. He stood upright, never turning towards me, and pulled himself up back over the ledge. Once he was up on the summit, covered in dirt, the security guard immediately went over to the edge and looked around. "Is there anyone else with you, kid?" he asked.

"No," Chris responded. He stood there stoically, now just facing forward toward the park, waiting to see what would happen next.

"Are you sure about that?" the security guard asked as he looked down into Chris' face, using his height and weight to intimidate him into talking. "I was told there were some girls over in the park. The park is closed now, and I didn't see any girls come down through the gates. So where are they?"

"I don't have any girls with me," Chris responded. "I am exploring the forest alone. I didn't know I had entered into a park."

"I didn't know I had entered into a park... SIR!" the security guard corrected. "Well it's not *just* the park, kid. This area is completely off limits. There is a 'No Trespassing' sign clearly labeled on that fence over there. No one is to be over here at all."

"I was just exploring the forest, and hiking around. I didn't know I wasn't supposed to be here.... Sir!" Chris replied, "It won't happen again, I promise."

"I am sure it won't, because you are going to come with me to the entrance, and we are going to call your parents." The guard put his hand on the back side of Chris' arm and pushed Chris in front of him, towards the security cart. I saw him walk away without any further protest, and he never looked back.

Chapter Nineteen
Under the Tracks

Once I heard the security cart pull away the parking lot and make its way down the hill to the entrance of the park, I found a way to scramble back up the cliff wall. As I was trying to pull myself up over the ledge, I heard Kevin and the girls coming towards me, and I felt Kevin's hands reach down under my arms. He helped pull me safely onto a flat terrain. I sat there for a second, letting the reality of the situation slowly make its way into my brain.

"What are we going to do now?" Andrea asked, sitting down next to me.

"I know, like, what *are* we going to do?" Erin repeated, sitting down next to Andrea.

"We are going to be in so much trouble. My parents are going to kill me," Andrea groaned.

"*Your* parents?" Erin asked in astonishment. "God, this is such a disaster. I wish I had never agreed to any of this." She avoided looking over at me at all, and then sighed, "Poor Chris... "

"Chris is cool. He won't tell anyone we were with him. Trust me," Kevin said with conviction.

His words of encouragement seemed to work, because the girl's began to relax considerably.

"Gwen, it's not your fault. It will be okay." Cat put her hand on my shoulder, standing above me. I wasn't sure why she said that, until I saw drops of water fall from my face and darken my jeans. Tears continued to stream as I shed the adrenaline and stress of the day. It had been a lot to take in for one afternoon. I felt so guilty about Chris being caught, that I just wanted to curl up in a fetal position and never get up again.

"Well, I wouldn't say that," Erin spat out. She was agitated, staring at me and pointing. "This *is* actually ALL your fault. What happened to Chris is *totally* your fault!"

"Erin, stop it!" Andrea burst out, hands up to her head as if she just couldn't take a minute more of any of it. She turned towards her and said calmly, "We *all* agreed to come here today. You were excited about it, remember? So just let it go already."

"I'm sorry, okay," I said as I stood up, wiping the tears from my eyes. I felt very alone at that moment, like my hold on reality was crumbling around me. "I don't know what else to do to make this any better. I'm sorry." I turned, put Chris' backpack on, and started walking along the edge of the ravine to the place we had ascended from.

"Maybe Chris will meet us down at the bottom by the time Mike is there to pick us up," Andrea asked hopefully.

"I am not sure how that can happen. If he doesn't tell them he is with us, how is he going to convince anyone to drive him to our rendezvous point?" Kevin asked, as he cinched up his pack and followed behind me.

"Come on girls, all we can do now is hike back down," I heard Cat say to Andrea and Erin. "If we're going to make it there by 8:00 p.m., we better get going."

I led the way, still wiping tears out of my eyes, feeling the weight of the world upon my shoulders. I noticed movement again within the shadows of the shrubs on the cliff face. This time I knew it wasn't Chris.

I made my way to our entrance point, and started to cautiously step down the incline trying not to slide. I could still make out movement out the corner of my eye, to my right: a shimmer of white amidst the shadows and was hard to focus on. Whatever or whomever it was moved away with each step I took.

Finally, after slipping and losing footing about a dozen times, fingers scraped, jeans scuffed, I came to a stop at the tracks. Still trying to focus in on the movement, I scanned the area to my right, now fully able to concentrate on the mysterious thing playing hide-n-seek in front of us. I heard the others slide their way down behind me, grumbling at the lack of footholds. Cat came up next to me, just as the full shape of the apparition fully materialized.

"Oh my god... Gwen. Is that Joseph?" she whispered in awe.

"You can see him?" I whispered back. "You can actually see him?"

"I *can* see him," I heard Kevin say quietly as he slowly came up behind Cat and I. It was as if we were all afraid of startling him; like a forest creature who could run off at any second.

"I can see him *too*," Andrea whispered in amazement.

"See! I wasn't lying. I wasn't making it up," I stated with a wonderful feeling of validation. He had come back to show himself, and I had witnesses. Everything we'd been through seemed to have been leading up to that moment.

"That is NOT a ghost," Erin stated as a matter of fact. It seemed being outside, even in the waning light, seemed to bolster her bravery. "It is just a little boy. Hey kid!" she yelled standing tall and defiant. "Come over here where we can get a good look at you!"

Where had that Erin been all day? I wondered.

The image began to shimmer and dissipate in response to her yelling at him, until he disappeared altogether.

"Wait. What? Are you guys *messing* with me?" Erin asked, looking at us confused.

Ah, there she is, I thought.

"You know, this isn't about *you*," I snapped at her, hoping my tone would put her in her place.

"This is *really* happening. It's been happening *all* day!"

"No, it just can't be," she stated again. "You're *lying*."

"Lying?" I asked dumbfounded. "Why would..."

Kevin interjected, "What did you think the *entire* purpose of today was, Erin? What has Gwen been telling us about for years?"

"You are all full of crap!" she spat, and turned away.

"How can you deny what you are seeing?" I cried out, shaking at her willful ignorance.

"Gwen, just forget about it," Kevin put himself between the two of us, "it's not worth it. Look over there..." he said, pointing over towards Cat.

"Joseph. That is your name, right?" she asked the pale figure reappearing amidst the shadows. Sometimes his features became clear, and sometimes they were diffused in a confusing play of light and shadow within the flora around him.

The little boy nodded. This was indeed Joseph. I got the impression that, up until that moment, I had been the only one to ever see him or acknowledge his existence. A sad smile lifted just at the edge of his mouth.

"Did something bad happen to you here, Joseph?" I heard Kevin ask him. "Is that what you needed us to know?" Joseph nodded, and looked down the length of the train tracks.

"Do you want to show us something over there?" I asked.

His pale figure made its way fluidly through the brush across the embankment of the tracks. He turned around, looked at us, and motioned us to follow. He turned, and started moving along the tracks back towards the zoo.

"You are NOT going to follow that kid are you?" Erin called out in alarm.

"This is the whole reason why I am here. I have to." I turned and started to follow the spirit down the tracks.

"I am not moving," Erin stated, crossing her arms in defiance.

"Wait for me!" Cat said, jogging up behind me to come along.

"Okay, wait up. You guys can't go alone," Kevin said as he jogged up behind Cat. I heard Andrea argue with Erin. I heard Erin complain and cuss about not wanting to be left behind, and then eventually I heard them follow up behind Kevin.

The sun was setting in the direction we were headed, so beams of light filtered through the canopy every now and then. It wasn't as cold as it had been in the morning, because the heat of the day saturated the still air. We could see bugs out in full force, gathered in swarms within the beams of sunlight.

The pale figure of Joseph disappeared around the bend of the tracks. When I managed to make my way around the corner, I saw him standing in the same place he first appeared to me. He was pointing at an area of ground.

"What are you pointing at?" I asked, looking at him, and hoping he could communicate better. "I don't see anything."

Cat looked around inquisitively, she replied, "I don't see anything that seems out of the ordinary."

Then I had an idea. I put my hand in my pocket, and pulled out the marble. I held it up to him. "Was this yours?"

His eyes widened, and he smiled. I could feel a shift in the air around me, like waves of happiness radiating around me. One second he was ten feet away, the next he was right in front of me with his hands outstretched towards the marble. I nearly toppled backwards from the suddenness of the transition.

As my heart settled back down, and I resumed breathing evenly, I displayed the marble in my open palm. He held out a frail translucent hand, his fingers trying to touch it, trying to grab hold. There was no feeling of physical contact, but I felt his essence flood into my mind's eye:

I saw through his eyes as if I was Joseph - playing marbles with my sisters. I felt pride at winning the Cat's Eye from the oldest one, and it became my most cherished prize.

I felt it, as I rummaged around in the deep pocket of my good trousers, as I stood at my father's graveside, and heard the horrible sounds of my mother sobbing. The smooth cold surface running around through my fingers kept me feeling happy on the inside, so I didn't have to see the sadness on my sisters' faces.

I kept it hidden in my pocket when my mother took me to a "church school" where my mother told me they would take care of me for awhile. She said my sisters would watch out for me, and that she would come to visit me every week until we would be back together again for good. But I was taken away from my sisters, and put in a building with all the boys. They were mean, and it was a very scary place. I cried every night. I would run the smooth Cat's Eye through my fingers to soothe myself, rolling it round and round reminding myself what home used to be like: what it felt like when my father came home from work, and lifted me high into the air spinning me around in circles, or what it sounded like when my father placed me gently down on the ground, and my sisters laughed at my wobbling about too dizzy to stand still. I loved the sound of my sisters' laughter.

I kept it in my pocket when they made me dress up to have my picture taken with some of the other children, and then we were put on a train. They told me I was going to visit a farm. I told them I didn't want to go visit a farm, because then my mother couldn't find me when she came back to take me home. I didn't get a chance to tell my sisters where I was going, so how would they be able to tell my mother.

For very long days and nights we rode that train, only allowed to leave once each day, when we pulled into a new town. Adults would gather to look at us, mumbling to each other, as we were made to stand in a row on the platform. We then were marched down from the platform, where the adults were allowed to inspect us. It made me afraid when those strangers would touch my face and look at my teeth, or check the muscles in my arms. I would yell at them and tell them to leave me alone. Holding the marble tight in my fist I would close my eyes and remember my mother and sisters' faces. I would yell that I just wanted to go home. My mother was going to be upset when I wasn't there for our visit. This made the people taking care of me upset. They would shuffle me back up the steps of the train, sit me back in my cramped seat and tell me to do a better job next time. They told me if I ever wanted to get off the train and visit a nice farm I had to mind my manners, stop sniveling, and show respect.

I still had my marble in my pocket when, at the last stop, the rest of us were chosen and taken to a large house high up on a hilltop surrounded by trees and farm fields as far as I could see. We were given over to Mrs. Briggs. She was a very strict lady, who told us all the rules we had to follow, before she took us up to an attic where we were to sleep. We were made to help out with chores around the house, or help the adults who also lived there, work in the fields. We were told we needed to be grateful for every meal she gave us out of the kindness of her heart, but that we would only be fed when she and her husband were satisfied with the jobs we were given.

I held on to it while I cried myself to sleep at night. I didn't understand how my mother could have let this happen to me. Why had she not come to take me home?

One day, Jane Elizabeth, Mrs. Briggs' only daughter, came up into the attic, pretending that she wanted to play. She did that sometimes, but she always got angry and ended up hurting someone. Sometimes, when one of

189

the children in the room got hurt or sick, they never returned. I am not sure where they went.

She brought up a tray, that day, with a teapot, cups, and a loaf of bread. She had us all sit around a table with her, as she poured us each a cup of tea and broke off a small piece of the bread. We were playing 'tea party'. When I told her the tea didn't taste good, she told me to dip the bread in the tea and eat it. So I did, because I was hungry and I liked that she was being nice enough to share with us. I started to feel sweaty and dizzy at first. I told her that something was wrong, that she needed to go get her mother. She told me there was no reason to, and that I should keep drinking my tea.

I saw one of the other children fall out of her chair, and she started to twist her body awkwardly. She was making scary noises, and again I told the girl she needed to get her mother. But then, the pain in my stomach suddenly hurt so bad, I doubled over and felt like I needed to vomit. A foamy liquid was dripping from my mouth as I bent over, my throat burned, my nose burned, and I could no longer see through the tears in my eyes. I fell over, and I saw my hand fall open... the marble rolled across the attic floor.

An awful smile spread across Jane Elizabeth's face as she picked up my Cat's Eye and placed it in the pocket of her apron...

Suddenly, I was looking down at myself... at Joseph lying on the floor. A man, with a long white beard and floppy straw hat, took our lifeless body from the attic and walked to the far edge of the farm, where he put our body in a hole. There were other lifeless children from the attic in the hole already.

We... he waited hoping that his mother and sisters would come for him... us.

"Are you okay, Gwen?" Cat asked, shaking me a little. "Is he talking to you?"

We... he watched as the zoo was built. He watched as the tracks were laid down over his bones, and he watched as the miniature train passed over them day after day.
I felt his loneliness and his helplessness when no one noticed him there.

"Gwen, can you hear me? Snap out of it!"

Until the day he saw me on the train, when we locked eyes, and he knew I could truly see him.

She shook me a little harder, until I felt the connection between Joseph and I fade away. I opened my eyes and could see him standing there as we held the marble together.

"Oh, Joseph, I am so sorry that happened to you," I said out loud. "I am here for you now. Do you understand? I am going to help you." The boy nodded.

"What is it? What is he telling you?" Kevin asked.

"That spot he's pointing at. He's buried there, with the other children, under the tracks," I answered. I looked at the embankment to see if there was anything to verify what he was saying.

"I can't believe we are actually seeing him. This is so unreal," Andrea mused in amazement as she came closer to where I stood. "How exactly are we supposed to help him?"

"He is still waiting for his mother and sisters to come for him," I said, tears falling down my cheeks. I looked at the faces of my friends. "What do I tell him?"

"Damn... That's a hard thing to have to break to the little guy," Kevin replied tenderly. I could hear the sadness in his voice.

"We need to mark this spot somehow. Someone has to come back here and find these children," Cat said as she started looking around for sticks and rocks.

Erin who had been standing off at a distance with her back to us, smoking, finally turned around to ask, "What are you guys even doing? Can we just go already? It's getting late!"

"We get it Erin... you are totally over all of this," Cat groaned. "Can you at least admit that *you* are seeing what *we* are seeing?"

Erin was taken aback by Cat's tone. "I don't see anything except you guys standing around looking stupid," she growled, stomped off to sit on a train track alone, and refused to acknowledge anything that was going on. "Whatever!"

"We can make a cross to mark the grave," Andrea stated as she started helping Cat collect items. Kevin began to pull up vines of ivy.

I stood there, watching as Joseph's little hand passed through my own in an attempt to hold the marble, and told him, "If your mother had known where they had taken you, she would have come for you. Your mother loved you. She only had you stay in that place because she wanted you to be able to have food and shelter. I know she meant to come back for you and your sisters, as soon as she could."

Joseph's face saddened, but I did my best to keep reassuring him that we would help. "That is what you want, right? To go back to your mother and sisters," he nodded in response. "Okay then we will get you there somehow. I promise."

"What is that going to be for?" Cat asked Kevin.

"We can braid the vines together and make rope. Then we can use the rope to hold the sticks together to make a cross," Kevin stated, as he continued to hunt for more vines. "We've got to hurry, we are losing daylight."

"Why braid the vines to make a rope? Just use the vines *as* a rope," Cat suggested. "It will be a lot quicker that way."

"Yeah, *Boy Scout!*" Erin yelled condescendingly.

In unison we all yelled back, "Shut up!"

"No, you're right. That makes more sense," he obliged.

Andrea leaned over to me and mumbled, "If you or I had suggested that he would have told us we didn't know what we were talking about, or something. Sheesh."

Kevin then took two of the longest sticks we'd then tied them together in the shape of a cross. He sunk it deep into the earth, right at the base of the embankment where Joseph had pointed.

"How are we supposed to find this place again?" I asked. "Maybe we can use these rocks to put like an X or something on the ground as well."

"Does anyone have anything colorful to help draw attention to this spot?" Cat asked.

I put down Chris' backpack, and rummaged through it. He had a red bandana at the bottom of the pack, and in the paper sack, with our garbage, were the left over foils from the Pop-Tarts. "I think we can do something with these, don't you?"

I looked around the area for a tree I could tie the bandana around, one that would stand out to us if we came walking back in that direction, but wouldn't be noticeable from the train. Finally I found a good candidate, and walked over to tie the bandana around the trunk of the tree.

I could see Joseph hovering just below the embankment watching us. "Joseph, would you like it if I left your marble here?" He smiled in response. I walked back over to the cross, and pushed the marble into the ground right at the bass, making sure it was deep enough that it wouldn't roll away. I noticed my watch then, and the time.

"Hey guys, we have a half hour to get down this hill. We have to hustle." I looked again at my watch, and then at Joseph.

"Joseph. This belonged to my favorite grandmother, who died a few years ago, I loved her very much." I took my grandmother's watch off, pulled out a loose Pop-Tart foil to place it into, and then pushed it carefully into the hole above the marble.

"That's a really cool thing to do, Gwen," Kevin said.

"I am putting the watch here with your marble, so that you know I will come back for you, and we will make sure you get back to your family." I covered up the hole as best I could, and placed rocks on top of the hole and around the base of the cross to make it more secure.

"We have to go right now, but we will be back for you," Cat said softly.

I was feeling the heartbreak again, the loneliness, the fear, the sadness… it was all I could do to tear myself away from his stare, and hope he understood.

Kevin turned away then and started down the hill, hacking away at the undergrowth with another large stick he'd found. Erin and Andrea followed immediately behind him. Cat lingered back, waiting for me, with her hand outstretched, and an empathetic sadness in her eyes.

"We will make this right somehow, Gwen, but we have to go for now." She turned, and pulled me with her back down the hill.

Chapter Twenty
It Didn't End Well

The trek down the ravine was much quicker than the climb up. In just a few moments, we'd half skipped and half careened through the undergrowth, kicking loose cascades of pebbles, tearing out chunks of moss, and ripping through fragile ivy tendrils. The forest closed back in behind us.

As soon as we were a ways down from the embankment, darkness swallowed us whole. We could no longer see the tracks or the house behind us, and there was no way to know where we were other than that we were heading down hill, fast. I could see Kevin's flashlight further down from me, swaying back and forth as he continued to machete the forest out of his way. He had quickened his pace, clearly aware that we were on a race against the clock. Andrea and Erin stumbled after him clumsily, while Cat and I trailed behind just as ungracefully.

"How are we going to get anyone to believe us?" I asked hopelessly as we continued recklessly down the hill.

"I don't know. We'll have to go back over everything we took, and see what we can come up with," Cat replied breathlessly.

When we finally tumbled beyond the edge of the forest canopy, the rich fiery orange twilight sky opened above us. A couple of cars, headlights blazing, flew past heading west up the highway. Something didn't look right. We stepped onto the graveled shoulder, trying to get our bearings.

"Crap," I muttered. "This isn't the same spot Mike dropped us at."

"Was it further up or further down?" Cat asked. "I am all turned around now."

"Kevin do you have anything left to drink?" Andrea asked, sitting down in the gravel. He pulled a Thermos from his pack and tossed it to her. Erin immediately went over for a drink as well.

"That's a good idea," Cat said, pulling her canteen off her belt. She unscrewed the lid and took a long chug, and then handed it to me.

"Thank you. Oh my god, I didn't know how thirsty I was." I gladly gulped down the warm metallic tasting water.

As I was handing the canteen back to Cat, I saw a set of headlights slow as they approached us, then the car pulled over onto the shoulder a few feet away. I covered my eyes from the glare of the headlamps to try and see if it was Mike's car.

"Gwenevere Iona Evans!" I heard my name bellowed from the driver side. Only one person ever used my full name like that... my father.

"Get your asses in this car right this second!" he ordered. "Andrea, Erin, your parents are on their way to pick you up from our house. All of you get in the car... now!" he yelled, and then he slammed the car door shut as he sat back down behind the steering wheel.

"Holy crap," Cat whispered. "Where is Mike?"

Andrea and Erin obediently made their way to the rear of the car, opened the door and slid into the back seat. Kevin scooted in next to them, and Cat climbed in to sit on his lap. I slumped down in the front seat, all too conscious of the angry stare my father laid upon me.

We drove in silence for a few minutes, until he had taken the exit off the freeway, and managed to turn around to head us back towards home. Only after we had hit a stretch of road that was a clear shot back to our neck of the woods, did the yelling begin.

"What the hell were you thinking?" he started. "What would have happened if one of you had gotten hurt? We had no idea where you were. You just took off for the day, and then we get a phone call from Chris' parents."

Ahhhh, now it made sense, I thought to myself.

"What do you think it is like to get a phone call asking if I knew where my daughter was?" he asked sternly, turning to look me straight in the eyes.

Clearly I have no idea what it is like, because I do not have a daughter, I replied sarcastically to myself.

"Chris got taken in by a security guard at the park and was given a ticket for trespassing. Are you happy about that?" he snapped. "Well, are you?"

"No, I am not happy about that at all," I responded, without making eye contact. I was actually relieved to know Chris was okay, and that he was home with his parents.

"Then when I got in contact with Andrea and Erin's parents, well the story just got better and better. Seems like you all lied to everyone, and I am the one who looks like a JACKASS because I didn't know where you all were."

"I am sorry, Dad," I replied quietly. With each outburst he managed to attain the desired result: to make me feel as small and as pitiful as possible, to take away all the excitement of the freedom we had for that one day, to steal all the satisfaction of our discoveries, to stamp down the wonder of the supernatural we had encountered, and to stuff me back into that box I had been in when I was first made to feel like the pariah of the park.

I wanted to scream at him that it was all TRUE. I had witnesses now, and we could prove it. But the more he yelled, the more I realized he would never believe me. What I thought, what I felt, what I knew… none of it mattered. To him I was a child: a child who had lied, and who had suckered all her friends into the lie, only to bring them into harm's way.

"Did you hear me?" he asked. "God damn it, Gwen. When we get home you are grounded for the rest of the summer!"

"What? Why?" I yelled back. I saw, over my shoulder into the back seat, how miserable my friends were. They looked like they wished they could just disappear. I immediately regretted yelling at him, but it was too late to take it back.

"The. Entire. Summer!" he said, emphasizing each word, like a hammer on a nail, for the greatest effect. I did not want to give him the satisfaction of a response, so I just ignored him, and stared forward the rest of the ride home.

When we pulled up to the house, I heard Andrea and Erin both mumble something under their breath. There were two extra cars at our house, one belonging to each of their families.

Cat and Kevin got out of one side of the car. Andrea and Erin exited out the other and then shuffled towards the house, like prisoners to a firing squad.

"Thank you for getting us home safe. Sorry for all the trouble we caused," Kevin said to my dad. His politeness took my father off guard, and defused his anger… a little.

"Oh, um, okay then. Do you need me to call your parents?" he asked Kevin. "You can use the phone in our house."

"No thank you, Mr. Evans. I can just walk from here." Kevin turned to Cat before my father could ask her the same question. "I'll walk you home," he said as he took her hand. She still held the puzzle box of keys under her arm.

"Are you sure, it is kind of out of the way. I can just call Mike," she offered.

"It's not a problem," he replied sweetly, then turned towards me to call out, "Take it easy, Gwen."

"You two get straight home then," my father grumbled, as he walked me up to the house. "Okay?"

"Okay... I'll call you, Gwen," Cat said waving good-bye as they walked down the driveway. I tried to wave back, but my dad had his arm around me moving us quickly towards the front door.

As we were just about to enter the house, Erin was being forcefully turned back around and ushered down the front steps by her dad. She didn't even look at me as she passed by, but her expression radiated pure hatred.

I tried to open my mouth to say something, but her father interjected, "I think you've done enough damage for one day, Gwen."

Inside the house, Andrea was sitting on the couch sandwiched between her mother and father - they'd been waiting for us. My mom was in the kitchen, avoiding the stressful confrontation. In true form, she would address me privately later, out of dad's ear shot.

"Gwen, what exactly happened today?" Andrea's dad asked me. He was making direct eye contact, using his lawyer tone. It was the tone he used whenever we did anything to disappoint him. I had known Andrea most of her life, and the two of us had done enough silly things in our childhood to cause that man disappointment. He expected us to behave like adults, to be rational at all times, even when we had been 5 years old.

"We went for a hike and picnic near the zoo. It was my birthday," I responded.

"Yes, that is the story you told us before, but why is it that you weren't with your parents, like you said? And why were there boys with you?" he continued, grilling me with questions. I looked over at my dad. He just sat there looking smug, happy to watch me squirm.

"I wanted to go with my friends, not with my parents. Besides they don't like to take me to the zoo anymore," I stated matter-of-factly, glaring at my dad in defiance.

"Why is it they don't want to take you there, Gwen? You don't have to answer that, we all know the answer," he stated, like he was in court. He might has well of said, 'Your Honor, there are no further questions. I rest my case.'

I wanted to scream at him, *I had not made anything up back then. It was NOT my imagination. It was NOT some desperate plea for attention. We had ALL seen him now, and I had proof.* I, instead, just sat there and kept my mouth shut.

I tried to tell Andrea, with my eyes, that I was sorry for getting her in trouble. She seemed mortified though, and wouldn't look up from her hands. She was twiddling her fingers together nervously, and bouncing her leg up and down like she was just thinking of a way to run out of the room before her dad could catch her.

"Well," he started as he stood up, grabbing Andrea's hand, "You won't be seeing each other for the rest of this summer, because Andrea is also grounded." Andrea gaped at him in shock. "You two are also forbidden from speaking to each other on the phone."

"What?" she cried out, before she could stop herself. "Dad! That's so unfair."

"*What* did you just say to me?" he asked, as he squeezed her arm harder and yanked her up from the couch, dragging her out the front door. I followed quickly behind.

I could hear Andrea whimpering and crying while she got in their car. As they drove away, I saw Andrea slump her head against the passenger window, visibly sobbing.

I thought, at that moment, I'd reached bottom. Every one of my friends was now in deep trouble, and it was my entire fault. I couldn't have felt worse.

"Are you satisfied with yourself?" my dad asked, as he turned to walk away into the kitchen. I bit my lip, trying to stop the tears that were coming.

"By the way..." my dad continued, "Where is your grandmother's watch? You didn't lose it did you?"

"No, I got it. Don't worry," I lied as I shut the front door.

That'll show me, I thought, *now I do feel worse*. I shuffled off to my room, dragging Chris' backpack behind me down the hall.

Chapter Twenty-One
Summer Blues

Normally, being grounded meant a few days of focused isolation, which usually fell apart when my parents became distracted with work or a previously scheduled family event. But this time, my father, humiliated once again by my "antics", seemed determined to hold the line. After a couple weeks of this forced seclusion, I'd begun to feel friendless and alone.

The only saving grace, the single ray of sunshine, that kept me from totally going off the deep end, was that by late summer we finally got cable at our house. MTV filled the void, and finally, the tedium of those long summer days with nothing to do was filled with entertaining videos. All the bands Kevin had talked incessantly about became my new favorites, and Martha Quinn was a friendly presence I welcomed into my living room each day.

Like most families in our town, we had no air conditioning, which meant this time of year I became a night owl. The sun didn't set until 9:00 p.m., and only really cooled down after that, so I stayed up as late as I could, and slept in as late as possible the next day. During those long night hours, I dwelled on every little thing, like what had become of Chris? What were the rest of them doing with their summer? I even wondered about Erin, even though I knew, when all was said and done, something irreparable had broken between us. At least I was able to take a sick consolation knowing that Andrea was probably as miserable, being grounded, as I was.

Each day, I greeted my incarceration with disdain as I was rudely awakened by the mid-morning heat, and as each long day passed, depression settled in deeper and deeper. It got to a point where I couldn't tell if I was just feeling that lonely, that sad, and that forgotten because I was still connected to Joseph, or if it was truly my own miserable condition.

I memorized the rotation of videos being shown each day and started counting how many times the same one was shown. I started to notice how bad the lip synching was, or how uncomfortable certain performers looked having to dance around. I was only pried away from my sick addiction for two hours each afternoon, so my mom could watch her soaps. Despite resisting at first, I got sucked into the story lines. I was disgusted with myself that I actually wanted to know what was going to happen next. When my dad got home at night, he immediately made me turn the channel, so that he could sit down with a cold beer and unwind to with the evening news. It was pretty much the same routine day in and day out.

I was only able to go out in public when my mom ran errands. She insisted I come along when she went to the pharmacy, the grocery store, or the post office, and said it was 'good to get out of the house'. I honestly felt that she didn't trust that I would stay off the phone, or that I wouldn't just run off to either Chris or Cat's house. Of course, she was right. If she left me in the car while she popped into some place for 'just a second', I fantasized about jumping out and running to someone's house, before she returned.

Could I do it? Maybe, I thought. *Would they find me? Probably.*

Eventually my dad relented, sort of, and allowed me to talk on the phone for small amounts of time. It felt like months that I had been separated from the real world. I could not wait a second longer. Finally, Chris and I would be able to speak to each other.

When he came to the phone, he seemed really happy to hear my voice. I was so relieved to know he was okay, but he had a rough go of it. He had to appear before a judge in juvenile court, and was sentenced to community service hours for the summer. He said, as long as he played along, when he turned 18 they'd seal his juvenile records, like nothing happened. He ended up working full day shifts out in the unforgiving summer sun doing grunt work for the city; mostly, picking up garbage along the side of the road.

I felt so bad! I apologized a million times for convincing him to go with me to the house, and thanked him profusely for helping us not get caught. When I asked him if he wanted to swing by and pick up his pack with his player and cassettes, he said he was busy. Something seemed off.

His end of the conversations became stilted, after that, lacking real interest, sometimes bordering on flippant. I asked what was wrong, and he always said the same thing, 'nothing.'

During this time I wrote hundreds of melodramatic poems, and commiserated with songs like: "Love Stinks" by The J. Geils Band, and "Only the Lonely" by the Motels. I wrote Chris letters while I sang these songs out loud, wondering what had gone wrong. The 'love affair', if it could be called that, had been brief but powerful, and its effect didn't easily fade. Worse yet, he didn't reply to a single one of my letters.

I was the only one to initiate our conversations; he no longer reached out to me on his own, which was hard to take. But one day things got even worse; each time I called his house I was told he wasn't there to take my call, and despite leaving messages, he never called me back.

Chris had always been my best friend.

The despair, over what might have been, and the confusion over what had happened, forced me to focus elsewhere as a distraction. I threw all my energy into obsessing over the documents and index cards stored in Chris' pack. Cat and I spoke as often as my dad would allow, and she said she had been catching rides to the library when she could, to look up more information about the Catholic Protectory and the trains that transported orphans from New York to the farms out west. At least, through her and me talking each day, working on the problem together, I was able to stay connected to the outside world and not lose myself completely.

We kept trying to figure out the best way to get authorities to dig for the bodies, but realized there was nothing we could say to convince a grown up to do that. We could admit we broke into the house, and that we found evidence, but even with that admission of guilt, the so-called 'evidence' was not compelling. It was only through my visions, and through Cat talking with her father's ghost, that we learned the truth about what the objects meant. To an outsider, nothing we encountered would make someone think there had been any wrong-doing. Nothing to justify digging up a section of the zoo's train tracks.

So what; there was a doll that was dressed to look like a girl in a portrait. So what; there was a medicine cabinet that had cyanide that could easily have been to kill rodents or pests. So what; there was a jewelry box of curious trinkets, which included teeth - small children lost teeth naturally, it didn't mean anything nefarious happened to them. So what; the children slept in the attic, they had to sleep somewhere. It was infuriating.

5

Cat snuck over to my house one night, when school was just around the corner, and tapped at my first floor window. She had called earlier and told me that she would ride her bike over. Despite it being well after dinner time, it was still light out.

"Come in," I greeted her quietly as I smiled ear to ear. My spirits lifted for the first time in over a month and a half. I lifted up the glass pane, careful not to make too much noise, and helped pull her up from the ground. "Good thing you don't weigh anything," I whispered, always astounded at how light she was.

Once she was in, we had a quick hug, and sat down on by bed to catch up. "So did you see Kevin today?" I asked.

"He's been busy most days. He spends his weekends doing some project, and also still works at the deli," she answered.

"Are you two doing okay still?" I wondered. She hardly talked about him anymore.

"I don't know. I mean we talk on the phone, but it's not like it was before."

"Yeah, I know what you mean. At least you get to *talk* to him. Chris has all but disappeared."

"Well, his parents pretty much have forbidden him from talking to you," she stated, as if this were common knowledge.

I involuntarily brought my hands up to my mouth, and muffled my surprise, "No! I didn't know that! Why would they do that?" His behavior suddenly began to make sense.

"Yeah, Kevin said," Cat continued, "they keep confiscating your letters, and made it really clear he's to have nothing to do with you." A look of sadness came across her face as she realized that I had spent all summer not knowing why Chris had rejected me. "I am so sorry you didn't know." She brought her arms in around me, and held me for a second, "I thought you knew."

After she pulled away from the hug, I sat there quiet, feeling sorry for myself, trying not to cry.

Cat changed the subject, "Remember, I was going to borrow the stuff we found."

"Did you find anything at the library?" I perked up a little at the change of subject, and the possibility of a breakthrough of some kind.

"Maybe. I am not totally sure, but I thought it wouldn't hurt if I looked at them for a while, with a fresh set of eyes," she smiled with a twinkle in her eye. I could tell there was more to it than that, but I had nothing left to offer, so I handed over everything I had.

"Have you gone back-to-school shopping yet?" I asked in a hushed tone. "Maybe my dad will finally let me out of the house to at least go shopping with you?"

"No, I haven't. I've been drooling over the back-to-school edition of the *Seventeen Magazine* though. There are the cutest metallic flats that I want so bad! Ask him tomorrow, and then call me. We can meet up at the mall and celebrate your first day of freedom."

"That would be so great. I've been *so* lonely and *so* bored, that I just can't take it anymore."

"Well, look on the bright side…" she began.

"There's a bright side?" I interrupted.

"Yeah," she whispered, "the summer is almost over. Freshman year at Carmichael High School! Dude, can you even believe it? We're ALL starting over. It'll be great." She gathered up the papers and index cards, and stuffed them into her book bag, "I have to get home. Call me tomorrow, you know… after your dad says yes."

5

The next day my father actually surprised me and relented… he would finally lift my house arrest. I was so excited at the thought of leaving the stuffy confines of my crappy little house, with the thick curtains pulled tight to keep out the scorching sun, and the hours and hours of mind numbing music videos repeating on my TV. I immediately called Cat and made plans for the next day. But later that evening she called me back.

"Gwen. Watch the news tonight. I just saw a teaser for a segment that's coming on. It is something I think you will want to see." Her voice was tight with excitement, like she could hardly contain herself. "I am not going to say anything else." Then she abruptly hung up the phone.

My parents were in the kitchen getting dinner ready, and I turned my attention to the evening news. I heard my dad calling out from the other room, "You never watch the news." He jested as he brought dinner plates out to set the table, "Are you feeling sick or something? By the way, you're mom needs you to help bring food to the table."

I switched between the major broadcast channels to see what news was being shown. "Just a second," I replied loudly as I stopped at each channel long enough to get an idea of what was being discussed. I switched to the next one, and the next one, and then made my way back to the first one. I did this cycle a couple times. I heard my dad tell me to come to the kitchen. I told him to wait. I clicked through the channels again… then I heard it:

The conductor of the Douglas Zoo train made a gruesome discovery today.

Chapter Twenty-Two
Unforeseen Hero

My parents and I sat around the television set, listening intently as the newscaster relayed in an emotionless voice the details of the discovery:

When asked about how he discovered the bones, the conductor said that several of the passengers brought to his attention a red flag waving in the wind at the top of one giant cross. The conductor passes that way every day and hadn't noticed it before. Staff from the Parks Department made their way along the tracks from the Douglas Zoo to remove the cross, when they discovered a hole dug into the base of the embankment with human bones sticking out. Local law enforcement and a forensic team were immediately called in to investigate.

'If that red flag had not been there, we would never have discovered the bodies.' The conductor told our reporter.

We followed up with an interview of the Douglas Zoo management and the County Parks and Land Division to see who would be responsible for the site, and what follow up investigation they had planned. Neither knew, at that time of this reporting, who was responsible for that part of the land, but the authorities had informed the North West Investigators of Archaeology to investigate the remains, due to its possible historic significance. We will have more news as the investigation develops.

I felt my heart lift out of the darkness it had been in for so many weeks. I wanted to dance for joy from the news that the bones had been discovered!

But how? I wondered.

"Huh, ain't that the darndest thing," he said, and then got up to switch the channel to 'Happy Days', as if it were just another mundane story.

I wanted to scream at him, *"Really? Really? That's it! No acknowledgement that it was in the exact spot I told you I saw a little boy?"*

Instead, I just looked at him. I was in awe at his ability to make no connection whatsoever between the current event and my past behavior… nothing. It was utterly amazing.

I got up, picked the receiver off the hook from the wall phone, dialed Cat's number, and then pulled the long extension cord into my room, where I could talk in private. She picked up the phone immediately, seemingly before it even rang. "You saw it?" she blurted out.

"Yes! How is this possible? I didn't tie the red bandana into a flag on the cross - it was tied around a tree. Who dug up the bones?" I had so many questions. Cat finally interrupted.

"It doesn't matter. I have a plan now," she said, so thrilled with herself, that she just started rattling off detail after detail of what we could do.

"And you know who we can get this information to?" I pushed further, trying to make sure the plan was doable, and would bring about the results we needed.

"Yes, but we have to do it tomorrow. School starts next week, and we won't have another chance. So tomorrow is the day we go "school shopping" at the mall, got it?" Cat conspired.

"Can we get to the office by bus?" I asked.

"Yes, and we won't have to waste most the day. We'll just drop it off, and let them do the rest."

"I can't believe we might actually pull this off," I said in excitement. "Okay, then, I'll meet you at the mall at 10:00 a.m. Bye."

I walked the receiver back into the kitchen and hung up the phone. I had no sooner hung up, when it rang again, startling me.

"Hello?" I asked.

"Gwen, it's me. *Oh,* my god, I just saw it on the news. Can you believe it? I mean, how great is that?" Andrea rambled on with excitement. "I can't really talk, I don't want my dad to know I called you, but I just wanted to let you know how happy I am that they found those bones. Talk to you Monday, okay?"

"Uh, okay! Hey, thank you for calling. I've missed you," I said.

"I've missed you *too.* This has been *such* a boring summer. Oh my *god,* we will totally catch up at school. Gotta go."

"Bye!" I heard her phone click first, so I hung up the receiver on my end. I glanced at the wall calendar next to the fridge, Tuesday was circled in a dark marker, and it read: *school starts*. I felt butterflies in my stomach. I had no idea what to expect, but it felt like it was going to be a whole new world.

5

Cat and I met the next day, at our designated time, out front of the Briarwood Mall at the bus stop.

We then waited for the bus that would take us by the local news station. Once we arrived we stepped off the bus and proceeded to walk up to the main door of the office. We pushed open the glass door, and heard a little bell ring as we entered into the lobby.

"Can I help you girls?" The receptionist called out from behind her desk, clearly confused at the sight of us.

We walked up to her and pulled off the best acting of our lives. Our story: we just happened to be walking down the side walk, and found a manila envelope addressed to that news agency.

"It has a name on it. Is that someone who works here?" Cat asked.

"Why yes! Oh thank you girls. We appreciate it. I'll make sure it gets to her right away," the receptionist said.

After leaving the station, we just stood there on the sidewalk taking the moment in, and then turned to grin at each other. It was the lightest I had ever felt. I was out from under the weight of the world and finally free of it all. It was out of our control from that point on, but we had placed it in the best hands we could ever have hoped for. She was the station's lead investigator, had won awards for her journalism, and she had a soft spot for righting the wrongs of history. For being the voice of those who could no longer speak.

"Cat, you are a genius," I sighed.

"I know," she gloated, playfully. "You want Baskin Robbins? I do!"

We took the bus back to the mall, and spent the rest of the day shopping, and hanging out in the food court. Finally unburdened, we were just able to chat like normal teens again, even discussing our classes the following week. It finally felt like things would go back to normal, even though we weren't quite sure what that new normal would be.

5

In the evening of Labor Day Monday, there was a knock on our door. My dad called out that it was for me. Having not been allowed visitors for what seemed like forever, I ran eagerly to the door.

To my surprise, it was Kevin. He stood there, all six foot something, in a t-shirt with a picture of Weird Al Yankovic holding an ice cream cone, with the song title "I love Rocky Road" written on it. He was smiling nervously.

I ran into his arms and hugged him tight. I didn't realize how much I'd missed him. "Hey," I said casually, as I pulled myself away from the awkward embrace.

"Hey, yourself!" he replied. "How've you been?"

"Better now. Come in, come in," I begged, hoping to catch up with everything.

"Sorry, I can't stay," he said, as he put his hand into his pocket. He looked up at me with his soft brown eyes and said, "I just thought you might like to have this back."

He pulled up my hand to his, and placed my grandmother's gold watch into my palm.

"Okay... so, um, bye." He then turned to go, leaving me standing there with my mouth agape.

"Wait! It was you?" I asked. He didn't respond, he just continued to walk down to his bike lying sideways on the driveway. "Aren't we even going to talk about *this*?" I questioned, holding the watch up in my hand.

Once he was mounted on his bike and had coasted out past the driveway, he turned and waved good-bye. The street lights began to flicker on in a slow procession throughout the neighborhood.

"THANK YOU!" I yelled, as I waved back enthusiastically.

"See you tomorrow at school!" he called back with a satisfied smile on his face.

To be continued...

{ Dedication }

This book is dedicated to my great-grand uncle Joseph Michael Pugsley.

After his father passed away in January of 1895, his destitute mother had entrusted him and his two sisters into the care of The Society for the Protection of Destitute Roman Catholic Children in the City of New York *aka* The New York Catholic Protectory.

He died in their care on the 10th of August in 1896, at the tender age of 6 yrs. 5 months.

Despite exhaustive searching, I have not been able to find his or his sisters' identification cards, and have yet to discover the actual circumstances that caused his untimely death.

As a mother of two boys myself, this family tragedy broke my heart. I felt compelled to tell their story, albeit through this fictional lens.

Thank You

To:
{The Urban Explorers, all around the world, for sharing their photography of abandoned places, especially Victorian Manors. It helped bring The Briggs' House to life.

{Riley Howard for our brainstorming sessions, and for taking on the challenge of creating my beautiful cover art.

{Angela Bennett for always encouraging my creative endeavors; acting as my first draft reader; brainstorming with me, and for your help with editing.

{Todd Downing for the read through, the thorough editing of the first half of the book, and for all your valuable ideas and advice in this process called "writing".

Last but not least:
{Paul Howard for your love and support through this life's journey, always encouraging me to find my muse, for all the long hours of in-depth critical editing, and for investing in my characters and the story they wanted to tell.

Find out what happens next in the upcoming sequel:

Beneath the Stairs

For more information:
https://www.facebook.com/g.howard.author

To learn the true facts behind this fictional tale check out:
https://gingerhowardauthor.blogspot.com/2021/06/true-events.html

Made in the USA
Las Vegas, NV
04 September 2021

29615362R00129